Operating Codes

Operating Codes

Nick Manns

Little, Brown and Company
Boston   New York   London

For Bel
who didn't give up

First U.S. Edition 2001

The extract on page v from *The Dhammapada,* translated by Juan Mascaró, 1973, Harmondsworth, London (page 35, lines 1–6), is reproduced by permission of Penguin Books Ltd.

Library of Congress Cataloging-in-Publication Data

Manns, Nick.
  Operating Codes / Nick Manns. — 1st U.S. ed.
    p. cm.
  Summary: Upon moving to Sentinel House, five-year-old Matty and fifteen-year-old Graham encounter ghosts from a nearby abandoned military compound, but real trouble begins when their father is arrested for posting information about a secret weapons system on the Internet.
  ISBN 0-316-60465-8
    [1. Trials (Treason) — Fiction. 2. Ghosts — Fiction. 3. Computer crimes — Fiction. 4. Conscientious objectors — Fiction. 5. Weapons systems — Fiction. 6. England — Fiction.] I. Title.

PZ7.M3165 Op 2001
[Fic] — dc21   00-054605

10 9 8 7 6 5 4 3 2 1

Q–FF

Printed in the United States of America

What we are today comes from our thoughts of yesterday, and our present thoughts build our life of tomorrow: our life is the creation of our mind.

If a man speaks or acts with an impure mind, suffering follows him as the wheel of the cart follows the beast that draws the cart.

The Dhammapada

Preface

by Dr. Theresa Davies, Clinical Psychologist at St. Margaret's Hospital, Craybourne

There comes a time in every physician's career when she or he is confronted by a case that is so baffling, so much at odds with notions of common sense, that they are forced to concede that science doesn't hold the answer to all the great mysteries. Well, at least not yet.

It is barely two years since the Hayton case made the head-lines; barely two years since the trial brought forth some of the most sensational evidence ever to grace the stage of an English law court.

Inevitably, because of the nature of that evidence, many people regarded the testimony as being the work of an over-excited imagination — and an immature imagination at that.

In the weeks that followed, who can forget the hundreds of newspaper columns that were devoted to explaining — or de-crying — the paranormal? Indeed, who can forget the number of celebrities who claimed to be in touch with figures from the distant past?

However, although the prosecution was to ridicule the sworn statement made by Mathilda Hayton, the youngest of the two children at the heart of the case, she has never privately or publicly gone back on what was claimed at the time of the hearing. Neither Mathilda nor her brother had a history of mental illness, and neither I nor my colleagues have been able to find any symptoms that might indicate delusion.

I have gathered together some of the clinical case documents* that were compiled in the months before the trial. They are a record of interviews and statements made by the children following their father's arrest. I have also included the celebrated letters obtained by Graham Hayton as part of his investigation that purport to throw light on the testimony of Mathilda.

Dr. Jay Carter of the University of Cambridge has stated that they are documents consistent with what is now known to have taken place in the immediate environs of New Barton.

Inevitably, I have received help and advice from a number of colleagues, and I would like to offer my thanks to Peter Westbrook and Catherine Heller of the Department of Psychology at the University of Southampton and to Dr. Gwyneth James of St. Margaret's Hospital.

I am indebted to Brian and Kate Hayton, Violet Thompson, and Keith Pyatt for their cooperation.

Theresa Davies
June 2001

*See Note on the Text, below.

Note on the Text

The main body of the text is provided by Graham Hayton. He worked on this narrative, with the help of David Lincoln from the firm William Scheiffer and Son. Graham made use of notes and tapes compiled at the time of the legal proceedings and has attempted, in his own words, "to tell what happened using only the evidence of my experience."

Mathilda's contribution is more fragmentary. The conversations were recorded over a period of weeks, and I have simply transcribed the interviews.

It is worth observing that during the period of conversation, Mathilda sometimes found it difficult to put her thoughts into words — either because of her immaturity or because of the emotional upset occasioned by the trial. However, her account is never less than compelling. And, as ever, it corroborates the statements of her brother.

The narratives have been interleaved for convenience. In some instances they duplicate each other; at other times they are an additional witness.

Graham did not have access to his sister's statements, before or after the trial proceedings. Nor did he read the transcripts while engaged in compiling his version of events.

TD

One

TD/MH: 4/19/99

MH My name is Mathilda Emily Hayton, and I live at Sentinel House, Potters Road, New Barton. I'm five years old, and my phone number is New Barton 738911.

TD My goodness, Mathilda. That's a lot of information. [pause] You're working on a painting. [pause] That's a very big house. [pause] Is that your house?

MH Yes.

TD Who lives in the house with you? [pause] Who's in your family?

MH Mummy. And my daddy.

TD Anyone else? Is there anyone else in your family? [pause] Do you have a brother?

MH Graham.

TD I thought so. Can you tell me how old Graham is?

MH Graham is, uh, fifteen.

TD   Thank you. That was very helpful. Can we look at your painting again? [pause] What's that next to the house?

MH   Those are trees. There's a path over there as well, but the trees, er, cover the path.

TD   Is that a kind of a — uh — lighthouse?

MH   No. That's a ro — ro — rocket.

TD   My goodness. You have a rocket on your front lawn.

MH   It's a pretend rocket. My daddy works on rockets when he goes to the office. That's his job.

TD   He's a rocket man. [pause] Right. And you've got some more trees there. And a car. What's that looking out from the window there? [pause] Is that a member of the family?

MH   That's [inaudible].

TD   I'm sorry, I didn't hear what you said.

MH   Ghost.

TD   Uh — ah, a ghost. [pause] Is that a pretend ghost? [pause] Mathilda. I was asking —

MH   No. The ghost is in the house. With us. [pause] It's real. [crying]

Two

It was a terrible day. Last autumn. The first leaves curling over, and three of us depressed.

We'd left Dad in the kitchen, the cell phone jammed to his ear, and joined the trail of movers lugging boxes down the driveway. Waiting patiently by the tailgate as bits of our lives were taken and shoved in position in that dark cavern. All the while Dad yelling abuse at Margaret Samuels, his personal assistant at Spere.

Matty was most concerned with her soft toy collection, I recall, and Mum had taken responsibility for fragile stuff — glass knickknacks, ornaments, that kind of thing.

Moving day.

There's so much more to it than simply shifting stuff from one place to the next. I'd spent my life in Nether Ashton. Been to school there. Learned to translate pencil squiggles into awesome graffiti in the boys' bathrooms. Learned to ride a bike without gripping the handlebars.

But this isn't a nostalgia trip.

Let's hear from the big man:

"*No. No!* I don't mean that, Margaret. That is positively *not* what I want. Look. Can you get Canine Video immediately and spell out the specifications? . . . What? . . . No. No! Will you listen to me for at least three seconds? . . . Yeah, yeah. I know that. I was the person who vetoed the decision in the first place. Look, Margaret, Believe me . . . Yes. Yes . . ."

The thing about Dad was that he was always so intense about work. I don't remember when the cell phone first entered his life, but believe me, it didn't make anything one bit easier. Not for him. Not for Mum. Not for any of us. It was like a portable stress machine. Whenever that little beeper went off, you could see the physical change that came over Dad. His shoulders would tense. He would lose any smile that was trying to find a way onto his face. He was immediately on all points alert.

Matty used to say that he had his Mr. McGregor face on, after the gardener in that book by Beatrix Potter, but I felt he looked messed up. The way I've seen quite a few teachers who work in our school look.

Technology was his life. It could have been his death. But that was later.

It was a bad moment for Margaret Samuels to call, because Dad had been busy supervising the moving guys — ensuring that the stuff was shifted in the right order, racing around to see that he'd put labels on all the boxes — you know, KITCHEN and SECOND BEDROOM lettered in bright red.

The one category that Dad wasn't trusting to the delivery people were the three boxes that he'd marked STUDY. That was because as soon as we "touched base," as he put it, he intended to leap out of the car with a box under one arm and the keys in his spare hand and open the house and immediately (I kid you not) start getting the fax machine plugged in and the computer wired up and so on and so forth. The whole bit.

This moving business made him insecure, I think. Not the actual departure from a home, but the temporary disconnection from the Mother Ship. I don't think he could conceive of effective communication without 240 volts and a dozen buttons to punch. So our home was packed up and put away, and after a last-minute sandwich, we were in the car and heading south.

It was after 3:30, and since it was mid-October, the sun was drifting toward the horizon. Matty had her eyes closed, listening to a Roald Dahl tape, and Mum had her face stuffed into a Stephen King horror story. Periodically, Dad would turn on the radio and then channel surf until Mum told him to stop.

"We're just going over the escarpment now, children," said Dad soon. This was a smart word for *hill*, but I was the only one tuned in to his travelogue.

"What do you notice about the vegetation up here?" he asked after a while. It was a question directed at me, because Mum was meeting the devil in Castle Rock, and Matty was in some other space-time continuum.

"There's not much?" I guessed, looking at the scrubby grass and wind-bent trees.

"Correct. Ten points," said Dad. "Why's that, do you wonder?"

And it was while I was reflecting on why there wasn't Amazonian rain forest covering this part of southern England that the first threads of mist started to drift across the road.

And very soon the weather changed. From cruising through a pleasant autumn afternoon, we were driving into a cloud bank. Dad stopped his interrogation, and Mum put aside her text.

"This is a surprise," she said, as Dad cut his speed so that we were crawling at about 20 m.p.h. We couldn't see anything in front except the yellow beam from the car's headlights. It was as though a great hand were pushing on the sky to suffocate the world.

"Do you think you should put your hazard lights on?" asked Mum after a while.

There was a long pause as we inched ahead, the only sound being the low rumble of the engine and the crunch-crunch of the tires on the road.

"Maybe," said Dad, leaning forward and peering into the gray murk. "It's not getting any clearer, that's for sure."

In a weird way it was like the whole world had been erased and we were left cautiously patrolling an alien landscape. Nothing in front; nothing behind. No trees, no stars, no people.

At which point, Mum jolted Matty awake with the exclamation, "What's that? There. Up ahead."

At first I couldn't make anything out in the great shifting nothingness, but then, taking form out of the fog was the shadow and then the substance of a man. He was standing right in the middle of the road, his legs astride and his right arm pushed out against us, the flat of his hand upraised. It said, Stop. It said, Go no further.

Three

"YeeaaAHHHH!"

That was the sound that woke me when Dad got the news about the house down at New Barton.

It was a Saturday morning, naturally, because on a weekday he's out of the place like a whirlwind and on the road dictating notes by 7:30.

"We've got it, Kate!" yelled Dad again, loud enough to unsettle the pigeons that were resting in the tree outside my room.

"Very good, Brian," said Kate obediently.

And then: "Daddy? — Daddy? Was that, was that — the dark house? Jenny said it was — uh — it had a ghost."

Silence.

The pigeons fluttered back to their posts, and I picked up my glasses from the bedside table.

"Well, I think Jenny is being a bit silly, Matty." I could imagine him picking her up and putting her on his knee. "It was a funny old house, wasn't it? Creaking and groooaaannniiiing!"

Matty giggled into her hands.

"I expect you'll creak and groan when you're a hundred and fifty-eight."

And she laughed again and then: "Don't!" she shrieked. "It tickles. Don't, Daddeee!"

I then heard the disgusting smacking noise that meant he'd given her a kiss.

She laughed, struggled, and he must have put her down, because the next thing, there was a rush of feet on the landing and her red face peered around the door of my room.

"Graham?" she said, coming to my bedside.

"I heard," I said. "We're moving into the New Barton house."

"Yes," she replied, sitting on the bed and looking toward the window. Then really quietly: "I was frightened. By the noises. Do you remember, Graham?"

Yes. I remembered. Of all the three zillion properties we'd been dragged around, this was the one that looked as though it had been designed by the makers of a horror film. You know: double gates at the road, a short gravel driveway, porch, exposed woodwork, double front doors. Dark.

The owners had already slipped off to someplace in the sun when we took a look around, so we were left with the energetic Mr. Pierpoint to do the tedious business of emphasizing the good and concealing the bad.

The previous owners, the two Misses Winter, were great conservers of electricity, so every room was lit with the glow of 60-watt bulbs. I'm not fooling. When I came out of that place, I had a headache that banged like a jackhammer.

Matty sat on the bed, looking at my book on steam engines. She flipped the pages and then said, "Graham, does the new house — the one we went to — have a ghost inside?"

The kind thing to tell a five-year-old was no, of course not, you only find ghosts in films and books; but then, I wasn't sure. So I said, "I expect the house is just old, like Dad says. You know, the timber and pipes and stuff aren't properly insulated."

"But it felt — it felt funny," she went on, looking up from the book.

It *had* felt funny. And that wasn't the only thing. While we were there, clustered together in one of the first-floor bedrooms, and as Mr. Pierpoint was describing the features ("You can see that even the glass in the windows is original, Mrs. Hayton. Imagine, we're looking through the panes that people dozens of years ago looked through"), there was a fizzing noise from the single bulb, and we were then dropped into a gray half-light.

No one said anything for a second or two. I think we were all surprised by the interference of something unplanned, but then Mr. P was able to make some comment about the bulbs being original features, too, and we shuffled off to look at something else.

So I said to Matty, as she sat on my bed, "Look, sometimes our senses play tricks on us. You think something is a bit odd, but really it's your imagination putting all sorts of strange ideas into your head."

"Okay," she said at last. "But that house doesn't seem" — she looked around the room for a moment — "friendly." And she slid off the bed and wandered away.

*　　*　　*

"What's going on, mate?"

Dad had lowered his window and was calling to the figure in the road.

He didn't move, didn't say anything.

"You know," said Mum, "he's a soldier. Look. I'm sure he's wearing a helmet, and that's webbing or whatever you call it strapped to his body."

She was right, of course. Because now that she'd given a label to his occupation, we could detect the traces of uniform, imagine the khaki cloth.

"Probably on maneuvers," said Dad, picking up his phone and punching in the usual machine-gun tap of numbers.

As he sat listening to the receiver, we all heard, faintly at first but growing louder as it got closer, the slow clinking and clanking of machinery. And then, inching up and onto the road behind the soldier, the dark outline of a tracked vehicle.

None of us spoke. The soldier didn't turn around or deviate from his station, and the tank made its painful progress across the road, its great caterpillar tracks pulling its lozenge of dark brown, as if a huge clod of earth had decided to cut its ties with the ground and go exploring.

"Of course, the weather has messed up the reception," said Dad, switching off the phone. "If it keeps on like this, we might as well check into a hotel for the night." He watched the slow passage of the army up ahead.

He looked at his watch. "My goodness," he said, "it's taken us an hour to cover thirty-five miles."

As he spoke, the vehicle vanished as completely as a pebble

dropped into a pond, leaving behind a falling cloud of exhaust and the soldier. He turned to his left, and walked back into the dark.

After that, as we moved ahead, the weather improved, and soon we could see the road stretching to the next hill.

We stopped at a café before Salisbury, and it was already dark by the time we passed through the village of Brenton Underwood and saw the nameplate that announced the hamlet of New Barton.

Sentinel House was beyond the other buildings, on the right-hand side. Our headlights caught the old gate as we slowly drove up the road to our house. They also picked up the heavy chain and padlock that secured the entrance.

"Now what?" said Dad, once more giving in to his well-developed sense of frustration. "I suppose it's back to Salisbury to get the key so that we can unlock the gate to get into the yard to gain access to the house."

"There isn't a key on the bunch Mr. Pierpoint gave you?" Mum asked.

"Why should there be?" asked Dad, his voice rising in tone. "There was no mention of a padlock or chains when we made the arrangement to move in. This is supposed to be a home, not a prison."

Nor a nightmare, I thought. But by this time, I felt it was probably worthwhile leaving Mum and Dad to shout out their differences. There was a flashlight in the glove compartment, and I persuaded a reluctant Matty to come with me and explore.

We crossed the road and climbed over the gate. Beyond the trees and bushes we entered a place of silence. The house was outlined against the lighter blue of the night sky, and it sat there, mute, heavy, and solid. Like some strange animal staring at us through the empty black holes of its eyes.

"I don't like this," said Matty. And then, tugging at my hand, she added, "Let's go back."

I turned and looked over at the car. Mum and Dad had the interior light on by this time, and Dad was busy with the phone.

I switched on the flashlight, its thin beam picking up the tufts of grass growing through the gravel. "No," I said. "Let's go and see what we can find."

We walked on three or four paces, and I stopped. "You know, it may be a bit scary, Matty, but there's nothing here to hurt us."

I'm not sure I believed my own reassurance, but I think a trace of conviction in my voice got through to her. She squeezed my hand, and we walked up to the entrance, my flashlight glancing across the dust-covered windows of the empty rooms. The door was, predictably, locked, so we stepped across the front toward the side gate that led to the garden at the back.

I'd just put my hand on the latch, had just touched the cold metal, when a huge face, all slavering teeth and dark eyes, leapt up out of the darkness and roared its fury at us.

Four

I dreamt of Dad that night.

We were walking up a grassy slope, he slightly ahead of me. It felt like early morning because the grass was wet. I could feel the cold of autumn, and there was the drone of cars on a main road.

The next moment we were standing beside one of the huge support chains that hold up the Clifton bridge in Bristol. I could see the stone tower of the upright rising into the mist. Dad stood by the chain, legs astride, wavy brown hair neatly parted.

He pointed behind him and said, his voice clear and confident, "This is the direct route to the best view in Bristol. Follow me to the top." And he turned and, leaning forward, stepped onto the chain and started his ascent, one foot in front of the other.

At one point he paused and looked over his shoulder. He shouted, "Don't look down! It's really clear up here."

Then he reached the mist and vanished. Not a trace.

Then I woke in a strange room.

There was gray light dribbling in through the blanket I'd pinned against the window, and I could make out my clothes and stuff heaped in a pile on the floor.

As the dream seeped away, I was left thinking about the incident that had frightened Matty so much — that strange meeting at the gated corner of the house.

The thing was, neither of us had heard anything to warn us of what was going to leap out of that darkness. The open jaws and the great roaring barks split the night like an axe.

The voice that followed didn't help much — "There, Joey, come on, good dog. Come on, boy" — because Matty had already run back to the main gate and was throwing herself over.

"Hello, my dear," said the figure, emerging from the shadow of the house. In the flashlight beam I could see that he was a bit older than Dad and was wearing a brown flat cap and duffel coat. "You must be the family that's about to move in."

It wasn't a question. He opened the side gate, and all I could do was nod.

"I'm David Thomas," he went on, holding the lead on the now-silent Labrador. "Sorry to give you and your sister a bit of a fright. The thing is, there was a whisper in the village that some transients were seen on the grounds around here, and I've been coming over each day to check for squatters. Last thing you want when you're going to move in."

Dad was climbing over the front gate by this time, and when we reached him, Mr. Thomas explained what had happened. He went over to the chain that had prevented the family's entrance and pulled open the lock.

"It's just a deterrent," he said. "I never shut the clasp, so you could've just opened her up and driven on in. The movers have been gone an hour."

He was a soft-spoken man, and his Welsh accent added to the odd feeling of the night. Like waking up in a house affected by settling: everything seemed slightly off-kilter — the world was still there but changed.

Which again was like Mr. Thomas's face. I wasn't really aware of it then, but later it was obvious that he didn't have full control of his facial muscles, so that instead of his features balancing, the left side of his face was pulled down, almost as if an invisible hand had grabbed hold of the skin beneath his chin and tugged hard. This exposed the lower lid of his eye, so that on cold days it seemed to fill up and water almost as if he were crying with some private sadness.

"Heard you were a computer man, Mr. Hayton," he continued, blind to Dad's evident desire to get in and switch on the real world. "Got a PC myself. Use it for games mainly, you understand. Do you play games at all? No, well I expect you'd be too busy.

"Just got a word-processing package and one of them things you use to send letters by the computer —"

"Modem," said Dad sadly, turning to look back as Mum brought Matty out of the car.

"Modem!" said Mr. Thomas. "Modem. That's the Jimmy, as my mam would say. Perhaps I could pay you a call — when you've got settled in like — and you might show me how a modem actually works? Not that I've got anyone to send messages to, mind."

And with that, he opened the double gates and waved himself off into the night.

We didn't do a lot of unpacking when we got in. The house was bitterly cold and, as before, haunted by strange echoes and odd sounds. It took Dad fifteen minutes to find the boiler and then another ten to figure out how to get the pilot light started. I was surprised that he hadn't plugged in the computer and asked for help on the Internet.

We spent the next week, the week of school vacation, "creating the familial infrastructure," as Mum put it (i.e., unpacking and cleaning and shifting stuff around).

Matty and I were given the opportunity to help out before we were dropped into our new schools, and Dad, well, once the study was wired and ready to go, he just carried on starting early and working late. He didn't leave at 7:30 to begin with, but then a major American client became interested in the software Dad's company was producing for the StarRaider, so he was rarely seen during daylight hours.

Sometimes there would be a sudden flare-up at Dad's long hours, and we'd hear raised voices and accusations late into the night. The point being that we'd moved to be nearer the office, not to continue with former habits.

But this isn't a tale of marital strife, as my English teacher Miss Crowther would put it, and I don't want to get too unfocused (as she would also point out).

So we'll skip the traumas of the new school and zip the clock forward five weeks. We're in late November now. The leaves have done their autumn stuff, and I've learned the complications of my class timetable. Dad was absent for vast swaths of time, and Mum was decorating the attic room.

The first odd thing I noticed as I trudged up the lane that Friday afternoon was that there was a guy in the middle of the road, under the streetlight, playing with a ball — lifting it in the air with his foot, using his thighs to keep it aloft.

When I got closer I could see he was about my age, with light brown hair, freckles, red sweatshirt, jeans.

He didn't take much notice until I was about to go past him to get to the gate, when he caught the ball in his hands and turned to me.

"Hey," he said, smiling, and I noticed his front tooth was chipped.

"Hi," I said.

"Moved into the house?" he asked, the ball now tucked under his arm.

"Yes." I stopped, and close up I could see that his hair had a slight orange tinge, so that the overall effect was a chestnut color. Auburn, I expect Mum would have said.

"Been empty for over a year," he said, looking over the wall at the house. "Been inside a few times myself. On and off."

"Yes?"

"Ye-es. Dad did some work for the Winter sisters. You know, plumbing, painting, that sort of stuff."

He dropped the ball to his feet and kicked it against the wall.

"Seen you at school. You're in Armitage's class."

"That's right." Yet I couldn't place the confident face of the boy now concentrating on tapping the ball against the brickwork.

"I've seen you a few times. On the bus and that. Catch it before you. By the shop."

"Right."

He paused. "So. Have you got a bike then? A set of wheels?" He looked at me, smiling.

"Yes. Nothing special."

"That's okay, then," he said, and he lifted the ball in the air, bumping it with his head onto the road. "I'll give you a call. I'm John Franklin," he added, and he trotted off, tapping the ball from side to side with his feet.

"I'm Graham Hayton," I called after him.

"I know," he said. "See you."

The second surprise was to find the Toyota sitting out front. It meant that Dad was home, even though it wasn't even four o'clock.

As expected, he was sitting in the study tapping away, but as soon as he heard the front door open, he stopped and came out.

"Graham!" he said.

"Right," I said. "I live here. Who are you?"

"Ha, ha!" he replied. "Anyway, I've had a great day at work and — how did you get on, by the way?"

"Oh fine, Dad, fine. Got caned a couple of times, and there was a fatal stabbing during the lunch break, but otherwise it was A1."

"Right!" he said, and he laughed in that great open-hearted

way of his, eyes twinkling. And then, as I followed him down the hall, he added, "It looks as though we're ninety-seven percent certain of picking up the Douglas-Knight contract for our software."

"Is that the American deal you were so interested in?" I asked. The thing being, if you've got a father who's a senior programmer for a large company, it's quite easy to lose track of the occasional successes he achieves.

"They're sending a team over in a couple of weeks' time, and I'm going to share the presentation."

"Is that like a special talk?" I asked, imagining something like school assembly going on forever.

"Yes, that kind of thing." He smiled, smoothing his hair. "You see, the purpose of the visit is to show some pretty tough cookies what our technology can do and why they should buy it."

"But the StarRaider isn't flying yet, is it?" I asked him.

"Well, there's what's known as a pre-prototype that we're using to test the avionics and so on. Anyhow, after tea, I'll show you something that will . . . will —"

"Blow my mind?"

"Well, possibly," he said, and he laughed again as he turned on the faucet to fill the kettle. His wide-eyed enthusiasm was touching: he was like a ten-year-old who has just been picked to be captain of the football team.

Mum was out with Matty at the supermarket, so I went upstairs and put *Viron* through its paces. If you've got one of the new games machines, this 32-bit "shoot 'em up" experience won't seem so hot, but if you need to let off steam, to fire and destroy incoming marauders, then it's the perfect end to an-other day at school.

I had never actually got much further along the line than the multigun laser fortress, but today I seemed to have lucked out and was annihilating the opposition like I was the captain of a helicopter gunship.

Dad had come up the stairs at some stage, I knew, because I sensed that he was standing behind me, looking down at the screen. But with three lives to go and 348,000 points showing, there wasn't time to discuss the latest triumph of the world's foremost computer expert.

"Yes!" I cried, as one of the immunity bubbles appeared and I was able to trigger a local nuclear holocaust.

In the space it took for the new landscape to form, I took a quick look to acknowledge Dad's presence; to say hi.

No one was there — just the long corridor, the worn carpet, and the dark pattern of the stained-glass window above the stairs.

Five

From out of the darkness
tumbling and turning
vapor rising from the upper surfaces
a scream of the future.

Cruising low over a forested plain
firing up into a vertical climb
contrails forming from the reheat of the engines
sunlight flashing on the light, on the flame
of the glistening cockpit curve.

The StarRaider

That shiny, sleek, shark-finned glimpse of the quick
the magical flick and roll of the jet plane
crossing and diving the ever-so-blue, ever-so-deadly sky.

Blasting at unseen foes
guided by heat
by the radar blip
by the touch of a button
and then
the rush and the flame
of the gray gunmetal flash
that surf these climbs
to impact with a gasp
of orange and black on some long-gone spot
dropping away from the blue.

We sat in the study. Listening to the voice-over; staring at a blank screen before we saw sunlight flashing up over the dark curve of the Earth and then the sudden shock of a high-speed aircraft roaring past at maybe thirty thousand feet.

Although I'm not exactly in love with the military, I recognized immediately that this was footage of the new plane. We saw it rifling into a climb, coming in at road height, rolling away from a pursuit plane, and firing a missile at an invisible target.

It was hugely entertaining, believe me, like enjoying a switchback ride from the vantage point of a camera lens. Or watching a carefully edited sequence of an air combat movie. The commentary supplied all the vital statistics, whether they were details relating to endurance or facts about its altitude capabilities.

Everything was hard and clear, and sitting with the rest of the family, I felt the reassurance and warmth of our shared lives. Matty had her head tilted to one side and Mum was holding the broken frame of her glasses in position so that she could follow the sequence. Dad stood to my left, the TV remote control in his right hand, obviously pleased with the demonstration. I could hear him humming his satisfaction, as images of the diving, swerving marvel were projected onto the lenses of his glasses.

And yet, a few seconds earlier, I had felt the foundations of my life shake — like my world was suddenly rotating on castors. For I *had* heard someone, and I *had* felt his presence behind me. And furthermore, I knew he was *so* close he had been pressing into the back of my desk chair. From that moment I was convinced that we weren't alone in the house and that whatever else happened, we were unlikely to remain alone.

Then Matty's voice dragged me back into the study: "Daddy, what does your plane *do*? Does it take people away — like — for a vacation?"

"Not quite, Matt," he said. "Let me explain." And he went over and sat on the coffee table in front of her. "It's what we call a *combat* aircraft. You see, if enemies come over a country to drop bombs on houses and families, then this airplane can go up and stop them from doing that."

"And how good is it?" I asked.

"The greatest leap forward in aviation technology since Reginald Mitchell decided on elliptical wings for the Spitfire," he said, and I could tell that he was now quoting from some invisible sales brochure. Like he was using us to rehearse his special promotion's spiel.

"What you have just seen is a machine that will fill order books and line runways wherever there's a country that needs an aircraft that is both low cost and high performance.

"And what makes that little beauty buzz, what makes it twist and turn and soar like a bird (and yet, what bird can fly like that?) is contained in the latest fly-by-wire technology stored in the binary code of the plane's onboard computers. Without them" — and he paused to allow all this stuff to sink in — "the craft drops out of the sky, unstable, unflyable even. But with the constant flow of electronic information, the digital dots and dashes transform twelve tons of hardware into a trans-sonic precision tool.

"This little beauty can detect and knock out a target smaller than my hand from a distance of over one hundred miles.

"This little beauty, using the latest satellite decoder, can be placed on the slipstream of a target that isn't even *within* radar range.

"And this little tool is kept aloft, twisting and turning by the binary codes contained in two three-and-a-half-inch disks. Imagine: from only three-point-two megs of instructions you've got a machine that can cruise the stratosphere at over two and a half times the speed of sound."

He turned around, flipped open the catches on his case, and produced a pair of computer disks. They looked pretty standard to me, and, except for a red strip running along the bottom, they could have been the kind of thing possessed by several hundred million households.

"These are the disks that contain the essential information for the aircraft," he said. "The bits of plastic that keep me working late at the office."

"So, so, those disks — or rather, what's on them is valuable?" I asked.

"Well, put it like this," said Dad. "There's fifteen years' work gone into this software. So you can calculate for yourself that these applications are worth more than a week's pocket money."

"But," I went on, "well then, isn't it dangerous to go walking around the place with them? You might be mugged, or we could be burgled."

"Yes, there is that possibility. There is such a thing as industrial espionage, but (a) I hardly ever remove them from the office, and (b) if they are being transported, they're kept in this" — and he pointed to his case — "which has reinforced steel sides and is secured by a Dragon Code lock."

"But you must have copies of the software at work?"

"Oh yes," said Dad. "But we still wouldn't like the knowledge to become widely available."

At which point Matty piped up with her tinny voice from the depths of her chair.

She said, "Is your plane made for killing people?"

It was like Dad had just been hit by a line drive. His mouth hung half open and he reached over to hang on to the computer monitor on his desk, as if to keep his balance.

"Well . . . ," he began, pushing his glasses up to rub his eyes. "Well."

"But what happens," she said, "what happens if the — uh — enemies buy the airplane? Won't they use it — to kill other people?"

Again Dad seemed to be stranded, as if the smooth speedboat of the salesman had suddenly run aground on a sandbank that had no right to be in the main channel.

He sighed. We watched.

"I suppose that could happen," he admitted. "It's a possibility. Sure. But the government sorts out who should get planes like this, and if they think the country that wants to buy the equipment is bad, then the sale will be prevented."

"But the airplane will *kill* people?"

"Look. Let's not get into that again," said Dad. "It's a very complicated issue, and, well, let's leave that for another day."

"But Daddeee," she persisted. "Mrs. Jones told us a story about Jesus, and she said that it was" — her brow furrowed with the effort to remember — "she said it was wrong to kill people. She said" — and again Matty paused, trying to extract the crucial piece of information from wherever it was stored.

"Well, you tell me what Mrs. Jones said when you remember it, dear," said Dad, pushing the videotape back into its box and opening his silky smooth black case.

"Jesus said you've got to *love* your enemies!" It all came out in one great excited rush. It had been the equivalent of carrying a heavy box up a flight of stairs, but Matty had worked at it and worked at it, and when she laid her idea on the table, I think she knew that she had presented Dad with an unexploded bomb.

Looking back on it now, with June sunlight pouring into my bedroom, it seems like Matty wasn't overwhelmed by the video and the polished talk, that she was asking all the right questions in her own naive way.

And other ears heard.

And other eyes watched.

Dad didn't reply at first, and Mum went out to start cleaning up the kitchen. I could hear her stacking plates and letting the water run hot.

But eventually, when the silence had become really uncomfortable, Dad turned around and sat down in one of the armchairs.

"This is really complicated stuff," he said, his eyes dark, his brows raised. "You're asking me very tough questions. Because, when it comes down to it, my company does develop products that are used in aircraft that have been used to kill people. There's no running away from that fact.

"But I also bring home a salary that helps pay for the house and the car and the nice things. And pays for the vacations that we have, and so on.

"I'm aware of what Jesus said, Matty. I'm not a religious man, but like everyone else, I'm trying to do my best for all of us."

Quite frankly I was surprised that he'd taken the whole thing so seriously. Usually with Dad a serious question got a jokey answer. Or a straightforward lie. But here he was being pinned down by a five-year-old who was quoting the Bible at him.

She didn't pursue her line of questioning. I don't suppose she had any more questions to ask, but I got the feeling that Dad wouldn't be given such a grilling when the suits turned up from Douglas-Knight.

I went to bed early and read an old American crime novel, where the crimes were obvious and the bad guys painted in bold colors. There was something comforting in this made-up world, because you knew that the villains were going to get put away and the private detective would get the girl. And best of all, you didn't have to puzzle out who to side with.

I don't remember turning out the light, but the next thing I recall was Matty anxiously, terrifyingly, tugging me awake. For outside, down below, in the empty courtyard was the sound of marching men stamping their feet in unison over the gravel.

Six

TD   Hello. How are you today? [pause] Did you watch TV over the weekend? There was a good movie on on Saturday. [pause] The last time I saw you, we had a look at a painting you were working on. Do you remember?

MH   It was the house picture.

TD   It was the house picture. You told me about the rocket and the trees and the path. Do you remember?

MH   [inaudible]

TD   I'm sorry, I didn't catch —

MH   The ghost.

TD   Yes, that's right. You showed the ghost looking out of the window.

MH   He was looking at me.

TD He was looking at you.

MH Yes.

TD Does the ghost live in the house? [pause] Do you know who it is? [pause] But you've seen him.

MH You can hear him moving around sometimes.

TD But you don't know his name.

MH He's not as old as Daddy.

TD Did he live in the house?

MH It wasn't his house. [pause] He stayed there.

TD Was this a long time ago, Matty? Did he stay in the house over a hundred years ago?

MH He didn't want to stay in the house.

TD Was he unhappy in the house?

MH [inaudible]

TD I didn't catch that.

MH He . . . he was alone. He didn't have friends. He was lonely. He had no one to help him, he had no one to talk to. [pause] He was in great . . . he was in danger. [pause] He didn't want to die.

TD Were there people who were hurting him in the house? [pause] Matty?

MH He said, Though I walk through the valley of the shadow of death I will fear no evil for thou art with me, thy rod and thy staff they comfort me.

Seven

The morning after the marching incident I sat opposite Mum at the breakfast table, watching her take a bone-handled knife and carefully slice the top off a boiled egg.

"Did you get back to sleep?" she asked after a while.

I nodded. My mouth was full of cereal.

"I'm going to let Matty sleep late," she said. "She was awake until after three."

"You said you never heard the noise?" I asked.

She shook her head. "You know me, sleep through a hydrogen bomb."

What *had* woken Mum and Dad was the sound of Matty's screams from my room, but by the time the light was on and my parents had arrived, the marching had gone and all we could hear were Matty's muffled sobs.

I explained to Mum and Dad what I'd heard, but what kind of sense can you make of a fifteen-year-old who talks about the sound of marching feet in the middle of the night? In the broad light of day, with Mum eating her way through a boiled egg and toast, and with a blackbird calling in the garden, the world seemed peaceful and calm. But in the dark, in a house full of odd sounds and whispers and with the unmistakable tramp-tramp-tramp of marching feet, everything seemed strange and threatening and sinister.

Dad had pulled back the curtain to look outside, but, with the exception of shadows thrown across the garden from the window, there was nothing mysterious in the dark.

"An aural mirage," he said after a moment and yawned. "It's to do with the density of the air. Like you can hear trains from quite a distance when it's a clear night, well, similarly other sound travels."

I thought about it for a moment. The red alarm clock on my shelf said 12:40.

"But Dad, who would be having a parade at a little after midnight?"

He shrugged. "Who knows? There are all sorts of army camps and bases and stuff around here. Why, you remember that tank we met on our way down?"

So midnight maneuvers it was.

After a while I said to Mum, "Do you think this house is haunted?"

She looked at me quickly and then wiped her mouth with a tissue.

"I think people sometimes put together different kinds of information and perhaps come to the conclusion that there are ghosts or whatnot in a building or place. Usually they're old houses and very rarely inner-city flats or new developments. And why is that, do you think?"

"Because old places have more of an atmosphere?"

"Yes," she said. "And because, as Dad said the other day, they tend to groan and creak more than new places. And also, everyone has seen horror movies and so forth on television. So when it's dark and creepy, we probably imagine more."

"I did hear the sound, Mum," I said firmly. "I don't know whether I was listening to the ghosts of men marching or that mirage thing Dad was talking about, but what Matty heard, I heard also."

And there was something else, something I hadn't spoken about. When I woke up, there was writing on the window.

Being a Saturday, it was a little after ten of nine, and I got up to see if there was a trace of the phantom soldiers. As I pulled back the curtain, I saw that someone had written in the condensation that clung to the pane. The letters spelled G-A-S . . .

There was obviously more, but the curtain had caught on the glass as I'd dragged it back, so all that was left was a word that didn't seem to go anywhere.

"If," I began, distracting Mum from her newspaper. "If there were such things as ghosts, what do you think they would mean?"

"Well," she began, and then added, "you'll have to accept, Graham, that I don't believe for one minute in the existence of ghosts. But given that, then I suppose you might put together some reason for their activities. Some people have said they're the spirits of tormented people who remain in the area where they suffered. Or you could argue that they're unhappy spirits who have a message for the living. In *Hamlet*, the ghost has . . ."

But she lost me at that point. She used to teach at a college, and, given half a chance, she'd be treading the boards as a lecturer again. I suppose chatting to Mum *was* comforting, but her reasonable voice didn't quite push away the fear of the night.

At which point, there was a loud rap on the kitchen door behind me. The kind of noise that might announce the arrival of the local police with a warrant to search the house.

"That's loud enough to wake the dead," said Mum, smiling.

Bang.

Bang.

Bang.

I got the ancient key and turned the lock — the lock of the door that opened up to the serious face of John Franklin.

"Hi," he said. "My bike's out the front."

"Oh, right," I replied.

After I'd done all the introductions and stuff, got my coat, and said I'd be back in time for lunch, et cetera, et cetera, I pulled my bike from the shed and walked with John to the road.

"Settled in, then?" he asked as we stood outside the gate.

"Oh yes," I said. "Just about unpacked all my stuff."

"Bit quiet for you perhaps?"

"No. We lived in a village in the north of the county, and that didn't even have a main road near it."

"Oh, you're well set up here, then," he said, staring back at the house, the suggestion of a smile touching the corners of his mouth. It was like there was some joke that he knew about but didn't intend to share. Some secret knowledge.

"Have you been to Wilson's Wood?" he asked after I'd closed the gate.

And when I told him I hadn't even heard of the place, he said, "Right. Let's go, then," and shot off out of New Barton in the direction of Craybourne. For a Saturday morning ride, he set a cracking pace. We went for about a mile, and I was glad that I'd worn my jacket, because it started to rain after ten minutes. A stiff wind slanted in from the right, so that I was soon soaked.

Eventually we came to a line of poplars that crossed the road, and John swung left onto the tree-lined track that climbed the hill.

He stopped and waited for me to catch up.

"There's a track around the wood," he said. "Like a cross-country trail. Plenty of hills and bumps to ride up over. Plenty of mud and water, too." He grinned.

The track between the avenue of poplars was rutted and puddled and used by vehicles of some sort, and horses, too. Their hoofprints stood out clearly in the pale earth. The green line of the wood could be seen rising over the brow of the hill, and when we reached it, I was glad to pause to catch my breath.

Once we were among the trees, it grew dark — the gray light falling onto the brown track that went off at right angles up ahead of us.

"If we go down thataway," said John, pointing to the left, "we'll come to the clearing and the huts. Let's go and have a look."

"Right," I said, wiping the rain from my glasses. "What huts?"

"You'll see," he said and pushed off, standing up to gather speed from his back wheel.

The track was obviously used by vehicles for taking away

felled trees or something. There were plenty of tire marks in the mud and puddles that looked deceptively shallow. I dropped abruptly into one and only just kept my balance, a brown slurry rising up my legs.

But John never stopped, never faltered. Through the gray mist of my smeared and wet glasses, I could see him in front, head down and pushing away.

The track swung in a gentle curve to the right, and I could make out a spur from the main route and some kind of fence in the distance. As we got closer I could see the shapes of several long huts, the kind you see in military bases.

"See you got yourself a soaking," said John when I reached him. "And I'm frozen myself," he added. "We can leave our bikes here and have a look at the old camp. Nothing much left, but you can find things. Like cartridge cases."

I looked beyond him at the chain-link fence. Someone had used the wire to string up the bodies of dead animals — stoats, weasels, rats, a squirrel. They hung there, sunken and decayed; their eye sockets pecked clean, their fur patched and thin.

Next to them was a white metal sign:

PROPERTY OF THE MINISTRY OF DEFENSE

IT IS AN OFFENSE TO TRESPASS ON THIS SITE.

KEEP OUT

"Are you sure it's okay to go in there?" I asked, a bit embarrassed by the question. Like being a five-year-old and saying, "I don't want to get in trouble."

Quite frankly, I've always had respect for signs that tell you to do this or not to do that. I used to get hot under the collar when Mum stepped into the crosswalk outside my old elementary school. And now here we were proposing to break into a place owned by the Ministry of Defense.

I said, "How do we get in?"

There was no obvious gate, and the fence itself — crowned with rolls of barbed wire — was at least twelve feet high.

"Well, we're not going to pole-vault if that's what you mean," John said, grinning. "You're not feeling a little bit — uh — chicken, are you?" he added, and he clucked a couple of times to demonstrate his meaning.

"Well," I replied, avoiding his direct stare and the sarcasm of the half-raised eyebrow, "it says it belongs to the Ministry of Defense."

"Ministry of Defense," he said, laughing, and spat in the direction of the animals, wiping away a trail of spittle that hung like egg white from his lower lip.

"We'll be okay. This place has been deserted for years. We'll hide the bikes over there, behind the bushes. Lean them up against the trees. And a bit farther on, where two bits of fence meet, there's a hole we can get through."

He smiled. "Don't you worry. Done this thousands of times. Really."

We propped the bikes behind some bushes and then went on for about a hundred feet. Occasionally we stopped when there was a rustle in the undergrowth — a bird or some small creature running away just to add tension to the enterprise.

The hole had been created by someone cutting through sections of wire close to the ground and then pulling back a triangle of metal. It was bent and curled over. I couldn't help wondering what hand had done this, and for what purpose. No one I knew would have had the interest or the equipment to force an entry into such a place.

But casting aside these thoughts, I followed John through, past some yew trees to an old path that led into the camp.

It was a place of silence and decay. The grass was long and yellow, like the lank hair of an old corpse, and our feet trod uneasily over scattered pieces of broken panes that lay over unknown mounds and bulges in the earth.

There were half a dozen huts, their windows gone, holes in their roofs. There was a ramp that must have been used for vehicle inspections and the site of what was probably a fuel depot: the pipes for the underground tanks were still there.

Otherwise, where the huts ended, there were just pieces of rotting wood, the ragged line of old walls, grass. It was like walking through the wreck of some sunken boat; the shapes of old life still clung about the place, but the spirit had long since gone.

When I looked around, John had disappeared.

"Hello," I called. "John? John!"

A pigeon flapped away from a tree beyond the fence, and a piece of cloth winked from a window frame.

"Oh, come on," I called out. "Stop messing around."

The rain came down steadily, and it suddenly seemed pointless to just stand in the open getting soaked, so I ran for the nearest hut, splashing through the mud and sodden grass.

There was no door, and debris lay in piles. As I crossed the threshold, I felt the hard prod of metal, and a loud voice screamed, "Halt! Who goes there?"

Eight

When my sight returned, I found I was on my back and staring at the broken board of an old ceiling. I could hear water dripping and smell plaster and dust. I had a headache the size of three counties, and I was cold. For a moment I had difficulty remembering where I was.

Slowly I got to a sitting position and felt for the epicenter of pain. My hand came back stuck with blood and hair.

The hut was empty. The rain had stopped outside, but there was a cold wind blowing through the doorway. Every slow movement hurt, but once I had my head resting against the nearby wall, I could sit with my eyes closed and wait for the tide of sickness to ebb.

Later I looked around and checked to see that no one else was present.

The hut measured maybe 250 feet by 50 feet. It wasn't difficult to imagine it crowded with beds and lockers and peopled with uniformed men, with a stove warming the area at one end and music from a wind-up gramophone at the other.

But now, after the weather and vandals, there were heaps of plasterboard, beer cans, and yellowed newspapers and magazines. Someone had started a fire on the far side, and there was an old can labeled Castrol GTX. It was the kind of place where people came to get drunk or to stretch out for a desperate night's sleep.

And all comers, all visitors seem to have added to the pictures and words that covered the walls. There were crude rhymes and cartoons of women, rival team slogans, and ugly scrawls about enemies and their relations.

But right next to where I sat, feeling the cool damp of the wall, was a sentence written in the style you sometimes see reproduced in history books — all loops and curls. It was neatly lettered in pencil, and it said: "Blessed are the peacemakers: for they shall be called the children of God."

It sounded like a kind of poetry — it had that sort of feel to it, the rhythm or whatever — and I thought it was from the Bible. It was at my eye height and carefully copied out — as if the writer was anxious that the message shouldn't be missed.

I have to say, I hadn't forgotten about John while all this was going on. I just had the leisure, once I could see straight again, to look around and to take in the environment. I didn't think John had belted me over the back of the head, but I didn't remember anything past the gruff voice and the prod of something in the chest.

Eventually, of course, I remembered that I had a bike and that it might be possible to pedal home. It was another ten minutes before I got to my feet, head bent with the lightning of pain that threatened to split my skull, and slowly shuffled through the door to the rear of the hut, to find the path that led to the fence.

Thinking back to that morning, crawling through the hole in the wire was the hard part. Bending down, getting caught on the bare metal and trying to unhook my jacket from its snag tugged at my last reserves of patience.

But my bike was still there, beaded with rain and leaning against the bush. I didn't attempt to ride it until I had gained full control of my legs. I was happy to steer a path between the trees and leave behind the memories of the morning in the camp on the hill.

I was just clear of Wilson's Wood when I saw a police car slowly coming toward me up the track that ran between the avenue of poplars. My mother, Matty, and John were in the back.

My mother was first out of the car. She was wearing her tan three-quarter-length coat, so I knew that she had left in a hurry. It was the coat reserved for four-star restaurants or a night at the theater.

"Are you all right?" she asked, holding me by the shoulders and looking into my eyes. "Where are you hurt?"

"I'm okay, Mum," I said, embarrassed by all the attention, and also by the presence of John and the law.

"John said you'd fallen and cut your head; that you were unconscious and that he couldn't bring you around."

"I've got a bit of a headache," I said, "but I'm okay, honest, Mum."

"Well, at least let me have a look at the injury," she said, parting my hair at the back. "It's difficult to see much because of the blood, but you've got an enormous bump . . ."

"I think we should just get home," I said. "Let's not bother going to the emergency room, Mum. It's not that terrible."

The policewoman stepped in at this point. "I'll just pop your bike in the trunk, Graham." And to Mum: "I'll drop you off at Wingfield Hospital. He's obviously been unconscious for more than a few seconds, so they'll probably want to give him an X ray to see that he's okay — and to check for a concussion."

So that was that. Police Officer MacAllister was a decent sort. She even got a message through to Dad to explain what had happened. Both the bike and John were off-loaded at Sentinel House, and we were then taken the ten miles to Wingfield.

Of course when we were alone, stuck in the emergency waiting room, Mum's wrath began to leak out. She wasn't prone to great outbursts of temper, but neither was she the kind of person to bottle up her feelings. "Your mother is very direct," Dad had once said, and I think he was referring to the quality of honesty she possessed.

She looked at me carefully with those clear blue eyes. "I don't know what you were playing, Graham. That area is out of bounds. There are signs saying "Keep Out" all over the place. The officer said that they have all sorts of unsavory characters drifting around there — tramps and alcoholics and heaven knows what."

I sat quietly and let her talk. I think she had probably been frightened by the unexpected change to her plans, and she was relieved that I was back in one piece. Matty was definitely happy. She squeezed my arm and told me that she was going to make me a get-well card as soon as we got home.

Yet when we got back and met Dad in the kitchen, he simply skipped the chit-chat: "I'm glad you're okay, Graham, but I can't hide my annoyance with what's happened. I had to cancel a meeting with the publicity director — who had given up tickets to a soccer game so that we could talk about the visit from the Douglas-Knight people — and all because you behaved stupidly.

"I've been up to the wood to look around, and" — forefinger jabbing — "I find the area positively spattered with "Keep Out" notices. I don't know if your mother has had a word with you about it, but what would have happened if you'd been knocked out and molested?"

"Brian — Matty's here."

"Right. I know — but you get my drift." His voice shifted down an octave. He touched my shoulder. "You're young, I know, but you've got to try and be a bit more — well, you know, responsible.

"And we've also got to be a bit more on the ball about security, Kate," he added, and he pulled his black case across the table, dark eyes looking up.

"What do you mean?" asked Mum, looking as puzzled as we all felt.

"What I mean," said Dad, "is that the window to the downstairs bathroom was left unlocked and was partly open. The alarm may have been switched on, but anyone could have gotten into the house. And I'm not sure that out here the alarm would have attracted the interest of anyone other than a couple of passing crows."

"I thought I'd checked everything," said Mum. "I know I was in a bit of a flap," she said, and she pushed aside a lock of hair that hung loose, "but I'm sure I saw to all the windows — upstairs and down."

"She *did*," said Matty, opening a food cabinet.

"Well, it must have come unstuck," Dad replied and strode off into the study.

"Someone's got a sore head," I added with as much point as I could muster, pouring myself a glass of water and reaching for the Tylenol from its perch on top of the microwave.

"Look, he's very preoccupied with this presentation," said Mum. "I don't know why they've asked him to talk to these people. They've got their own sales staff at Spere. But we'll be entertaining two American gentlemen in a couple of weeks' time. And maybe Dad's boss."

"Who's he?" asked Matty, her hand deep in the cookie tin.

"That's Mr. Fletcher. The man —"

"The man who hands out the orders," I added, heading for my room.

I fell asleep during the afternoon. I didn't take up Mum's offer of lunch, and when I woke, my mouth tasted of sour milk; there was a pain over the bridge of my nose where my glasses had entrenched themselves and an ache that radiated from the back of my head. Otherwise I felt great.

It was just past four, the sun tipping its hat in the direction of the west, when the doorbell rang.

"Your friend is here," Mum called up the stairs, and for a moment I wondered whom she could mean. It had to be John, of course, but why would he want to come back after the shenanigans of the morning?

"You okay?" he asked when he came into the room.

"Fine," I said, gesturing toward the chair by the table.

"Nice room you got," he said, looking around and, ignoring the old tea chest stuffed with junk by the wardrobe, touching the box of game disks by the computer.

"S'okay."

"Did they give you a lot of grief at the hospital?"

"No. Nothing like that. The pain's eased up."

"Good," he said and let the conversation stumble to a halt. I flipped on the bedside light.

"What do you think happened, then?" he asked eventually.

"I must have slipped or something when I went into the hut. It wasn't your fault, you know. You gave me a shock and everything by shouting out, but I fell over. I wasn't pushed."

As I was speaking he turned from inspecting our back garden and listened with obvious surprise at the narrative. When I finished, he startled me by saying, "I don't follow you."

"Uh — which part?" I asked, wondering whether I'd been especially vague in my explanation. To be truthful I felt tired and fed up and wanted the sickening day to end. The bang on the head hadn't been a picnic, and I resented the telling-off from Dad. And somehow I held John responsible. If he hadn't been messing around, hiding and so on, then none of it would have happened.

"Well, you said something about shouting out? What's that supposed to mean?" He flipped through the floppy disks. Tap-tap-tap.

"Look," I said, closing my eyes and thinking back over the events. "I called you, and when you didn't answer, I figured you were hiding, so I ran to the hut to get out of the rain. Well, you know, as I walked through the door, you said something like, "Stop. Who goes there?" and prodded me with a stick or something and the next thing was lights out."

He looked at me for so long I thought time had stopped.

"That didn't happen," he said eventually. "I was poking around among a pile of trash at the back of one of the huts. Thought I might find a cap badge or belt buckle, you know. I heard you calling, but I didn't come straight away, didn't think there was any rush."

He stopped for a moment, looking to his right out of the window. "When I turned the corner of the hut, well, you weren't there. I thought" — and he smiled at the memory — "I thought you might be playing some kind of trick, you know, hiding or something like that, but you weren't.

"I saw your legs as I got level with the doorway. To tell you the truth, I thought you were dead. It was really eerie. No one there. The hut empty except for you. I could see the whites of your eyes under your lids. I thought you were kind of looking at me, but then it was obvious you were out cold. I had to bend down and listen to your mouth, to see if you were breathing. But I didn't hit you."

Nine

Monday morning started in Judaea.

A certain man went down from Jerusalem to Jericho, and fell among thieves, which stripped him of his raiment, and wounded him, and departed, leaving him half dead.

And by chance there came down a certain priest that way: and when he saw him, he passed by on the other side.

And likewise a Levite, when he was at the place, came and looked on him, and passed by on the other side.

But a certain Samaritan, as he journeyed, came where he was: and when he saw him, he had compassion on him.

And went to him, and bound up his wounds, pouring in oil and wine, and set him on his own beast, and brought him to an inn, and took care of him.

And on the morrow when he departed, he took out two pence, and gave them to the host, and said unto him, "Take care of him; and whatsoever thou spendest more, when I come again, I will repay thee."

"Well, students, there you have a story that was told two thousand years ago in the Middle East. It's about a man who was beaten up and robbed. About people who wouldn't go to his aid, and about one man who didn't even come from that country who helped the injured person and took care of him.

"And when it comes to *your* turn, students — and Vincent, I'm looking at you — when it comes to your turn, and your friends say, 'Let's go and take the new boy's bag for fun,' what will you do?

"Or if you find someone who isn't the most popular person in your class who needs help, will *you* be the person who provides it, or will you be the one to look away and pretend that nothing has happened?"

I wasn't really giving Mr. Parks much attention, I have to admit. Assemblies, particularly on a Monday morning, are times when I find it easier to tune out and think of more pleasant things — the weekend's soccer match or what's on TV tonight. But the Good Samaritan assembly reminded me of Dad in a strange way.

The story seemed to be about someone who was mugged by bad guys and how the people who wouldn't help him were just as bad, and the thought stumbled into my head — for the first time — that it could just as well be about *Dad:* for what was he other than best friend to a gang of bad guys? If you earn your keep helping warplanes to fly, then surely — surely? — *your* finger is just as much on the trigger when it's time to start shooting?

*   *   *

After break we had geography with Mr. Hardcastle.

"All right, students," he began, "quiet down a minute and I'll tell you what's on the agenda today."

Like all teachers, he had these little phrases and mannerisms that he tended to use and repeat. He came from the north somewhere, and this, too, gave an edge to his speech. Lessons always began with him explaining what was *on the agenda;* we were always *lads and lasses,* and when he had to rebuke some student, the delicious word used to describe misbehavior was *malarky.*

"Right," he went. "You'll find you've got an extract from the Craybourne survey map in front of you. Er, you'll find it easier to follow, Ramage, if you turn it the right way up. Thank you. Okay, as I was saying, on the board there are twenty features that I want you to locate and identify. You've got twenty minutes for this little exercise. I'll come around and give you a hand should you need my personal assistance."

Quite frankly I always regarded geography as an exercise in common sense. You know: Volcanoes bubble up because of magma — a hot porridgelike substance — finding a way to the surface. Rivers flow quickly when there's a steep hill; they tend to slow down when there isn't. The sea usually wears away rock. But you get the picture.

Today there was purpose in looking at the settlements and the wandering veins of the road system because the map featured Wilson's Wood and the old camp.

I let my eager-beaver classmate Martin Adamson work his way through the list, while I studied the local area. The wood was green and marked with brown contour lines. It was much larger than I had at first thought, and, as I knew, it surrounded the army camp.

The track from the road was marked as a red dotted line, although the map hadn't included the trees that bordered it. On the far side of the wood was the path of an old railroad that had once connected with the main line going to Craybourne. The railroad seemed to have come to an end at the wood, or at least the track didn't go any farther.

The shapes of huts in the camp were marked in brown, and across the area the words DANGER were inserted in red.

"Okay," said Mr. Hardcastle, "we seem to be having a problem locating a dry valley. I don't think you can be looking very hard. There are at least three examples that I know of."

There was a footpath that left Wilson's Wood in a south-westerly direction, went under a high tension line, and then curved back, over the contours to New Barton. The footpath from the old camp came out on the road almost exactly opposite Sentinel House. The camp and the house were linked on the map.

And it occurred to me then, sitting in that classroom, that I was looking at the route into the past.

I met John at lunchtime. He was with a group of guys on the back tennis court, playing the usual game of soccer.

"You got a minute?" I called, as he muscled his way through the defense.

"No!" he yelled when he'd shot wide.

But after an insulting five minutes, he strolled over and leaned against the wire, all the time watching the game.

"That head of yours better?" he asked, and then shouted, "Hey! Scotty, Scotty — come out, get out!"

"Fine," I said. I didn't know where to pick up the conversation. "What, uh, what did you make of the business in the hut?"

"Oh, you mean you thinking that someone was there when there wasn't." He laughed. "To tell you the truth, Gray, you had me going there." He snorted and nudged me in the ribs. "Made me laugh, quite frankly. You were only kidding, weren't you?"

"Well, not really. What I said about the man and everything actually took place."

"Well then, that bump on the head must have shaken up your ideas, you know, knocked your brain box. I'll get it," he called, and walked off the court to fetch the ball.

And when he came back: "Perhaps what happened was that you ran in, slipped on the wet floor, and dreamt that someone had attacked you."

"Look," I said. "There've been some odd things happening since we moved in. I thought I'd do some nosing around. Try to get to the bottom of it. You game?"

He ran forward and booted the incoming ball across the pavement.

"Goal kick!" he yelled against the cries of protest. "Depends. What'll it involve? Not hours down at the library?"

"No, no," I hurried to reassure him. "Nothing like that. Just a bit of digging around. That sort of thing. Interested?"

"Maybe," he replied, stopping to check his watch. "I'll catch up with you, Gray. It's twenty after. Time for lunch."

I wandered over to our home room, thinking again about the voice that had rung out the challenge last Saturday at Wilson's Wood. Could it have just been some vagabond sleeping in the camp? Or was the meeting connected to all the other stuff that had invaded our lives? The stuff that didn't make any sense but that seemed to keep leaping out at us wanting to be heard.

When I got off the bus that night, Mum and Matty were waiting at the stop. Before I had a chance to say, "What are you doing here?" Matty ran up and shouted, "Look, look what I found, Graham," and she held out a dark object that was hanging from her neck by a piece of string.

I took it in my hands, holding it out under the streetlight, so that I could see what she had.

"It's a badge," said Mum. "She went into the garden as soon as she got home and was busy playing near the wall. She said you'd be interested. Probably off some soldier's uniform."

"Do you like it?" asked Matty. "We can share it."

Ten

TD/MH: 5/3/99

TD   Hello, Matty. The last time we met — a week ago — you were telling me about the person you called the ghost — in your house. Do you remember the conversation we had?

MH   [inaudible]

TD   You said that the ghost was a man. [pause] You said the man was frightened.

MH   Bad men wanted to hurt him.

TD   Who were the bad men?

MH   They had old clothes.

TD   What kind of old clothes, Matty? [pause] Were they wearing — like — rags, clothes with holes in them?

MH   They were, they were wearing brown clothes.

TD   Were they wearing the same kind of clothes, Matty? Were they in uniform?

MH   They were soldiers. Old soldiers, but they weren't
       old.

TD   They were from a long time ago.

MH   Yes.

TD   Did they live in your house?

MH   There was a king.

TD   A king was on the throne.

MH   [inaudible]

TD   And these soldiers — the men in uniform — wanted
       to hurt this man.

MH   Yes.

TD   Why was he in danger?

MH   He came to my window.

TD   He came to your window?

MH   In the night. I woke up. There was a noise — like
       scratching. The light was on outside. The light was on,
       so that I could see to go to the window.

TD   Did you pull back the curtain? [pause] Did you look
       outside?

MH   It was nighttime. I wasn't frightened. There was the
       light, and I went over to the window. I pulled the cur-
       tain. I couldn't pull it all the way back because it
       stuck. I saw the room and the door behind me in the
       glass and then I could see my face looking out
       and . . . and . . . where my face shone in the glass was
       the face of this man. He was looking at me. He was

tired. His hair was dark. It was really wet, like he'd been standing outside in the rain. He wasn't as old as Daddy. And I felt so bad that I started to cry. Not loudly, but just like crying, and I could see my face in the window, and I could see the light and the door behind me, but the man wasn't there.

Eleven

I was stumbling down a muddy track through a forest of elephant grass. I could feel sweat dribbling down my back, and more trickled into my eyes. I could taste salt. Then I entered a clearing, the earth packed hard and brown and dry — like it was used for a meeting place, or something like that.

Mr. Parks from school was sitting at a desk in the middle of the open space, writing a letter. He looked up as I came toward him. He smiled and said, "Take your pick, Graham," and pointed out two paths behind him, each disappearing into the undergrowth. One was marked FLIGHT and the other FIGHT.

And then the door of the bedroom opened, and a stranger walked in and flipped on the light.

"Okay. It's two-thirty in the frigging morning — a Tuesday morning — and I've just had the misfortune to be woken up. And do you know why that is? Have you any idea why I should be wandering around the house at this time of night on the day when I have to leave the house before six in order to get everything together to participate in the dry run of next week's presentation to the team from Douglas-Knight?"

Dad was standing in the doorway, hands on hips, wearing his red-and-black-striped pajamas. When I'd gotten my glasses on, I could see that his hair looked a mess. His face was screwed up like he was in some kind of pain, and the shouting went on. And on.

"I mean, what in heaven's name have you been telling Matty? I mean, what's gotten into you? Do you do this deliberately? She's five years old, for heaven's sake. Five. She's been on the planet sixty-odd months. Now she's seeing faces in the window. I mean, Graham, she's sitting on your mother's knee crying her heart out. Convinced that the dream she was having was real.

"I mean, I know that you have talked to your mother about your concern that this property might have the odd ghost in it, but your mother's old enough and sensible enough not to listen to your half-baked ideas.

"Maybe I'm being a bit unsympathetic here, maybe that bang on the head you sustained the other day has affected your judgment. But quite frankly, Graham, what *really* disappoints me about this episode is that I thought you were too smart for this kind of stupidity. I thought you realized we'd progressed a bit beyond medieval thinking. You know, drawing ludicrous conclusions about things that go bump in the night.

"As far as you're concerned, from now on, the only thing that will go bump in the night is me when I'm mad at you.

"And in the future, in the future" — he was stabbing his finger in my direction — "don't ever, *ever* talk to Matty about hearing ghosts or seeing ghosts.

"If you still believe this half-assed nonsense, then I'd better make an appointment for you to receive psychiatric help."

He paused at this point, and I knew it was over. He was simply looking for some way to make an exit.

"But no more," he said finally, holding his hand up. "I've got enough on my plate without these — interruptions."

And with that he switched off the light and walked out.

Fear came wide-eyed and cold as soon as he'd finished speaking. I lay there as the dark eased, listening to all the odd noises of the house settling in the night. Waiting for the sound of feet outside, for the door to open, and for something to come toward me that was not of our time.

It's easy to smile about it now, but later, when I was in the witness box and struggling with questions, I wondered who else had been watching that night.

I thought about the whole episode during the bus ride to school the next day. John was sitting with his friends at the front, so I had the chance to reflect on Matty's experience, Dad's reaction, and the soldier's badge.

It was about the size of a half dollar. Although it was dark green with dirt, I could make out a crown mounted on a shape that was similar to a Maltese cross. There was a raised circular plate in the middle that contained some sort of pattern, and the whole design rested on a scroll that probably contained writing.

"Why don't you clean it?" Mum suggested once we'd gotten back.

"How do we do that?" I asked.

"Yes, Mummy, yes!" said Matty, getting excited.

Mum took the badge, scratching its surface with the sharp point of a curved nail. "This is probably made from brass," she said after a while. "At the moment it's all dark and covered with grime, but if you get some metal cleaner" — and she bent down and rummaged in the cabinet under the sink — "and let it soak overnight, that might help."

Before school (and after Dad had long gone), I walked through the wet grass, beyond the apple trees to the brick wall. There were an old compost heap, a metal bucket with a hole rusted in its bottom, and the ashes of a fire. Among the cinders there was the usual junk you find in such places: bits of broken glass, rusted, half-burned cans, some unrecognizable pieces of metal. But there was nothing further to connect this place with the army.

I took the badge with me to school.

And had to wade through a morning of graphs and the problems of the Bennet family in *Pride and Prejudice* before I could get up to the history department.

"Right," said Mr. Pyatt when I discovered him. "That's a pretty disgusting specimen of a familiar cap badge."

He was an old man with white hair and strong blue eyes. He had been teaching history since Nelson was a boy, and when I introduced myself, I got the impression that my name was of less importance than the contents of the lunch box he was inspecting.

"You haven't parted with serious money for that heap of junk, have you?"

"No," I replied, irritated by his valuation.

"That's just as well — Graham, is it? — because it's not worth anything. They made hundreds of these. Thousands even."

"Oh," I said.

"And do you know where you'll find those thousands now? Where the greatest collection of military badges can be located — hmm? Eh?"

"I'm not sure," I said.

"No, I don't suppose you are. Not even an educated guess?" He paused, once again looking up from his desk.

"The Tower of London?"

"Hmm, not bad. Shrewd, but entirely incorrect. Look, I'm going to give you a great clue now. The biggest collection of these things can't be found in Britain. They're not in this country at all! So what do you say now, Sherlock?"

Not in this country at all? And there are thousands somewhere else?

"Might the badges be on the remains of soldiers who died in a war?"

His face lit up like a nuclear explosion. It was as though I'd just beaten the record on a TV quiz show. "You know, Graham," he said at last, "that is an excellent deduction, excellent. And you're not even doing honors in history — what are you taking?"

"Geography."

"Of course," he went on. "Geography instead. So you give up a subject that would have tested your intellect and you end up spending your time considering the oxbow lake and the hanging valley. Now, let's get back to business. This piece of metal.

"This is the cross of the Wiltshire Regiment. The scroll at the bottom, if you could clean some of the garbage from it, would say as much. These badges came into use in the eighteen eighties. And they were worn right through both world wars. Take a day trip to Bethune or Bapaume, and dig down a couple of feet in the nearest field, and I bet you'd uncover one of these."

"So, these were worn by soldiers in the First World War?"

"Exactly. Steel helmets didn't come into fashion until the war was eighteen months old, and until then your average soldier had little to protect his brains except the normal regimental hat — with one of these" — he tapped the badge — "at the front.

"So, tell me, young man" — and he looked over the top of his glasses — "where'd you get it?"

"My sister found it at the end of our garden."

"Ah," he said, and he seemed disappointed. "Not France, then? Probably discarded by some boy at the end of hostilities. Interesting though."

And for a moment he turned his attention back to his sandwiches.

"He'd have looked like your man over there."

And he gestured with his hand toward the long bulletin board.

And there he was — a soldier sitting at one of the desks by the window. His hat was pushed back slightly, so that I could see his hair. His face was streaked with dirt, and his hands, resting on the table in front of him, were dark with mud and filth. He was unsmiling, gray, still.

Twelve

A trick of the light? An optical illusion? The delayed effects of the bang on the head? I don't know. But for a brief moment, held in the dust floating in that still air, there was a soldier, worn out by the routine of death on the Western Front, seated on the second floor of the school.

"Mr. Pyatt —," I said.

"Yes," he said, looking up.

But by then, even as I began to speak, all that remained were the floating motes, the sunlight, and a black-and-white photograph blown up to poster size and pinned to the bulletin board.

"Oh, nothing. I — I just thought I saw something."

"Ah," he replied. "Of course."

I went over and examined the picture. Close up, a lot of the definition seemed to have washed out, and it was less focused. I ran my fingers over the smooth surface.

I turned and saw the teacher staring at me.

"I think I might be suffering from a concussion or something. I had a bang on the head a couple of days ago. I" — I pointed back at the poster — "thought I saw something over there. Like — I know this sounds crazy. It was like the soldier had come to life."

"Really?" said Mr. Pyatt, opening a drawer in his desk.

"I wouldn't think anything of it, but so much strange stuff has been going on at home."

There was a long pause. He looked at his watch. He said, "Like what?"

It took about twenty minutes, I suppose, but I told him everything — about Matty's vision at the window, about the sound of marching in the night, about the incident at Wilson's Wood. He was a good listener, pushing away his lunch box and letting me tell the story from the moment we'd first visited the house. Occasionally he stopped me to check on a detail — "Matty saw a face?" "What exactly did you hear in the hut?" — but otherwise he was silent. At the end, when I'd completely finished, he said, "Did you say you lived at Sentinel House?"

And when I confirmed the fact, he added, "Most curious, hmm, really," and he made a note in his diary. It read "New Barton??"

"Well, there's obviously a lot we don't know," he said eventually, looking at his watch, "and we've got barely ten minutes before the bell rings and civilization rushes to an end. But," he added, looking straight at me, "it might be — uh — helpful, if you could find out the history of your house: who has lived in it; if the local people know anything about it; and so on. But" — and he touched my arm — "I would be inclined to go easy on your long-suffering parents. If your father has a demanding job and he's preparing for some big presentation, then I'd try and be a bit — uh — discreet?"

I nodded.

"Good. So, let's see," he said, and he pulled his blue appointment book from the pile of exercise books on his desk. "It's Tuesday now. Why not come and see me at about this time — uh — next Tuesday? Should give you time for research and give me time for thought.

"Oh — and by the way," he said, as I was just going through the doorway, "you might like to find out why your home is called Sentinel House."

Quite frankly, it had never really occurred to me. There was the name, chipped out of the stone on our gateposts, carved into the lintel over the front door. There, but strangely invisible.

Sentinel House.

When I look at it now, it seems obvious what its associations are, but then? It was during science class that I borrowed Adamson's dictionary. *Sentinel* nestled between *sentimental* and *sentry:* between the tender and romantic and the watchful and suspicious. A sentinel was a soldier who guarded a military establishment. Someone who was watchful and suspicious rather than tender and romantic.

I thought this over on the bus ride home. Looking out over the gray December landscape, I realized that, for whatever reason, our contact with the military stretched from the past and was now invading our lives.

And as for the figure in the classroom — the worn-out, dirt-covered soldier? He *had* been there, as strongly and as certainly as the tables, chairs, books, and chalk dust. He had sat listening and observing and yet had faded as surely as smoke drifting on an autumn afternoon.

It was with this jumble of thoughts that I crunched up the driveway to our house and inserted the key into the lock. As I did this, the front door swung back, and I was left looking at the twisted smile of Mr. Thomas.

"Oh," he said immediately. "I hope I haven't given you another fright. Haven't brought the dog with me this time, though, so you're all right. Come in, come in. It is *your* home, after all."

Thirteen

And as he laughed, one side of Mr. Thomas's mouth went up and the other came down. I wondered whether he hadn't been involved in some kind of accident, some work-related disaster that had twisted his face like a punched balloon.

"I just came by on the off-chance your dad might be in. Hoped to pick that brain of his. Find out how to get my modem up and running."

Mum and Matty came up behind him as I crossed the threshold.

"I can help you with the modem," I said suddenly. "If it's just a matter of plugging in, getting the software loaded, that's not a problem."

"Oh, the wonders of youth!" said Mr. Thomas, smiling at Mum. "I was born forty years too early!" And he paused, as though a thought had just struck him. "I suppose you couldn't borrow your dad's computer to show me how you send and receive mail, could you? I mean, I know I might give the impression of being the original blockhead, but, although I think I can probably get the software side sorted out, I'd like a run-through with the application."

"Suits me," I said.

"Would that be all right with you, Mrs. Hayton?"

"I'll make another cup of tea," said Mum, already turning and walking down the corridor.

And from Matty: "You took the badge to school. You did!"

And she stamped off before I had time to explain.

The study is on the first floor at the front of the house. From the bay window you can look out over the driveway toward the gate and to the road beyond. Like all the other rooms, it is broad and light with a high ceiling and a fancy plaster rose in the center.

The farther wall is lined with books, and Dad's table — an ornate brown affair that he picked up in some warehouse in Craybourne — faced the door. There is a worn leather sofa and an old armchair.

It was the kind of room that you can imagine would suit a doctor or a lawyer or some other professional person. There was a slight smell of age about the place — a mixture of books and old cigar smoke, I suspect.

But the surge protector and the tangle of wiring from the monitor and computer spoiled the effect. As did the startling graphic that was framed over the fireplace: the StarRaider.

That day I wasn't entirely comfortable about entering Dad's territory — it wasn't just *any* desk after all with its pots of clips and pens, its piles of paper and box of disks.

I could imagine Dad's disapproval — the raised eyebrows,

the dark look. "What do I need for protection," he'd say, "garlic and a crucifix?"

But I took Dad's place and switched on the power, listening to the whirr of fans and the clicking of the hard disk. Mr. Thomas was looking at the files on the bookcase.

"I forgot your dad was in the airplane business," he said, staring at the StarRaider.

"Well, that's just a part of his work," I said. "He's a computer programmer — you know, he puts together the code that makes things work in particular ways. You've probably heard about the StarRaider project?"

He nodded, touching the disks on the desk.

The screen came into focus. "There's the desktop. There's the e-mail application. You double click on the icon to load the application. Like so."

At which point Mum came in and placed two mugs on the table.

"It was three sugars, Mr. Thomas?"

"Exactly right, Mrs. Hayton."

There was a kind of oiliness about him that I wasn't comfortable with. Ordinarily I like the music of the Welsh accent, but with Mr. Thomas — slippery, that's what he was. And sharp, too. I got the impression, as he sat next to me and I went through the procedures for sending and receiving mail, that he knew it all anyway.

I'd just gotten to the bit where you can hold down CONTROL and SHIFT in order to monitor the progress of messages, when he gave an exclamation and his mug of tea was rolling away on the carpet.

"I'm *so* sorry, Graham," he said, standing up. "I was so taken with your tutorial that I knocked the tea off the table."

"No problem," I replied, knowing very well what my father might say. "At least none of the papers got wet."

"Or the disks," said Mr. Thomas, looking at the box parked near the screen.

As he didn't make an attempt to go into the kitchen and ask for assistance from Mum, I picked up his mug and said, "I'll just get a cloth, Mr. Thomas, if you'd like to take a seat."

Although I've never heard Mum bad-mouth another adult in my presence, I realized by the downturn of her mouth that she was less than enthusiastic about our visitor.

"It might be just as well to keep this to ourselves," she said. "Your father's got enough going on to raise his blood pressure without this mishap." She paused. "When's he going, anyway? He was here an hour before you arrived. Get rid of him, can you?"

I was as good as my word.

I blotted the carpet with the kitchen towel and then tapped and clicked through the closing procedures at rather less than novice speed. "And there you have it, Mr. Thomas. You'll be able to send electronic messages right around the world now."

He stood up, smiling his crooked smile down at me. He touched my shoulder lightly and said, "You've been *very* patient, Graham. And I must apologize once again for the mishap with the tea."

And then nodding toward the StarRaider on the wall, he added, "It's appropriate that the military should be returning to this house. The Winter sisters were a bit of an aberration."

I followed him to the study door.

"What do you mean?" I asked.

"Well, I don't know all the details, the background and whatnot, but Sentinel House used to belong to the army. Not in my time here, but certainly until after the Second World War. The Winter sisters bought it subsequently. I believe they might well have had some military connection themselves — you know, father in the army, something like that."

He turned on the doorstep. "Thank your mother for her patience. If I need further help I'll know where to come."

Fourteen

Two days later Dad was on the six o'clock news.

Just after the twenty-minute news summary, the newscaster announced the first successful flight of the StarRaider from the British Aerospace factory in Coventry:

"This is the result of a fifteen-year collaboration among four European partners and promises to provide work well into the twenty-first century," she said.

There was then footage of the plane making a steep ascent from some anonymous strip and then further glimpses of its slippery form as it made a cautious circuit below the altostratus.

Inevitably, the firm and decisive Defense secretary talked about how splendid it all was, and then there was Dad, in his navy pinstripe and red tie, grinning into the camera.

"The key to this aircraft," he said, in response to a prompt, "is the onboard computer. Airplanes have made use of instruments ever since the Wright Brothers launched their craft in North Carolina a century ago, but the StarRaider is different.

Take away the computers, and the plane simply topples out of the sky: it's inherently unstable."

"But what's the point of that?" asked the interviewer.

"Well" — and he smiled at the invitation — "if you want a highly maneuverable aircraft, then you need to make it so that it can respond with rapidity to complicated instructions. Human beings do not have the quickness of thought or the deftness of touch to carry out the tasks that are second nature to a computer. This aircraft" — and he gestured to the taxiing form behind him — "can outfly anything that has two wings and an engine."

"And so, there you have it," said the correspondent, face to the camera. "As the new century begins, we now have an aircraft that can't be flown by human beings yet can outsmart enemy aircraft. This is Michael Redfern, BBC News, at Lindon Airfield."

We were sitting in the living room — Mum, Matty, and I — and I think we were all relieved that everything had gone well. Although Dad had known about the interview for some time — the managing director of Spere was out of the country and Dad was thought an appropriate choice — there had been panic that morning.

I was woken by feet thundering up the stairs and Dad shouting, "Look, Kate, I can't hang around. They were in a manila folder with a red spine."

"And you left them on your desk?"

"*No!* For the last time, I didn't leave them on the table. The folder was resting on top of the computer books immediately behind my chair. I put all the stuff together and left it there last Sunday evening."

There was the sound of feet going down the stairs and then more voices from the study.

It was the kind of situation to stay away from. When Dad got into a state he lost the ability to reason: vision and hearing crashed, and concentration — that desktop of calm — became a whirlwind of overload.

Yet he was fortunate in having Mum to help him through the crisis, because in situations of this nature she was rarely inclined to panic. She would quietly ask the appropriate questions and then get going on the methodical work of sifting through the evidence. You could tell that she was a policeman's daughter.

All this before six o'clock in the morning.

The stuff turned up, although, curiously, in two locations: the performance specifications were on the bookshelf, and the rest of the folder was propped alongside the collection of *Scientific Americans*.

"Thank God!" I heard Dad say.

"Amen to that," added Mum. "And you better get going if you're to pick up Tim Foster en route."

And that was that. The next time I saw him, he was beaming out of our twenty-one-inch TV, looking for all the world like a calm and capable human being.

They were to use the same footage during the trial.

The following Saturday, which would have been December 5, I agreed to go into Craybourne with Mum and Matty to pick out a jacket. Although Mum wasn't "hung up on appearance," as she put it, she felt that denim had too much of the street corner and too little of the three-course meal about it. And since I was to be present when the Americans arrived next Thursday for the social get-together, something tailored was the order of the day.

Anyway, that Saturday, when I awoke at my usual 7:13, I could tell that there was a thick blanket of snow on the ground. It felt like the house had been wrapped in bandages during the night. When I looked out at the garden, the bushes, lawn, and rainwater barrel had become vague shapes — as if some busy chef had tripped over a flour sack.

When the phone rang at 10:30 I was ambushed by an unexpected voice.

"Ah, Graham," he said. "Enjoying the precipitation?" It was Mr. Pyatt. "Look. I won't keep you. Just a lead that you might like to follow up on before we meet next week. There's a Miss Violet Thompson in New Barton. An elderly woman who apparently wrote a history of the town twenty years ago. According to the telephone book, she's at number six Underwood Lane. Might be worth talking to. Have a peaceful weekend! Bye."

And he was gone like a figure disappearing in a blizzard.

An hour later we were in Craybourne: a freezing town filled with pushing, shoving, bad-tempered shapes, stumbling in their bulk through slush, unbalanced by the packages they carried down the wet paths.

But we waited patiently in the line for short-term parking and then calmly proceeded to the department stores and the fitting rooms. We were able to maintain this Buddhist detachment because we'd left Dad behind at the keyboard. In fact, none of us saw him that morning — just a distant grunt before we left the house. And without his preoccupied self, we were able to carve our path without the need to get it all done quickly and without having to constantly check that his pager was working or to duck into alleyways to call his voice mail.

And it was also library day, so after we'd chosen some clothes and before we stopped for a burger and shake, we dropped our books off at the library and agreed to spend twenty minutes looking through the shelves.

There are a couple of computers in the library that people use to access the county database. This is a fancy way of saying you can use the system to see what books were written by particular authors and whether they happen to be on the shelves of your own library or at some other branch.

Mr. Pyatt had mentioned that a Violet Thompson had produced a history book about New Barton, so I carefully typed in her name and hit RETURN.

Believe me, it's an old system, so I had to be patient while it did its stuff. The green lettering remained impassive while the various electrical switches went searching for a match.

And then the main menu disappeared and a text and author frame rolled up.

It hadn't discriminated about Thompson, Violet; the whole of the Thompson catalogue was thrown on the screen, but there, dead center, was the entry:

THOMPSON, VIOLET, *NEW BARTON:*
FROM DOMESDAY TO DALEKS, 1976

There was only one copy, but the good news was that it could be found in the Reference section under Local History.

Yet when I went to look in the appropriate area, there was no such book by Miss Thompson. There was plenty of stuff about Old Craybourne and local industry, about wildlife and conservation, but no *Domesday to Daleks*.

This was because pamphlets and curious texts not produced by mainstream publishers were locked away in a glass-fronted cabinet. I found this out when I went to ask a woman at the information desk.

"Well, dear," she said, a booming Scottish accent breaking the stuffed silence like a brick, "if you come with me, we'll see if it's been put where it's supposed to be."

Four minutes later I was sitting with the other researchers, flipping through the eighty-two-page pamphlet in search of references to the camp at Wilson's Wood and the presence of the military in New Barton. And this is what I found, after perusing the index:

Just after the end of the Boer War, in 1904, the War Office established a small research center on the hill in what was known as Wilson's Wood.

This is a remote part of the county, two miles beyond New Barton in the direction of Craybourne. The camp was never to become a site for the employment of local people, as was the case with the larger establishments to the east — at Tydeworth and Bulkington — and rumors proliferated as to what was going on "up yonder."

The military maintained a presence until 1956, when there was an announcement in the local press to the effect that the War Office had deemed the base "surplus to requirements" and closed it the following year.

    Although the government has always refused to explain what use was made of the facility, the elaborate preparations made for withdrawal and closure — which included both the demolition of buildings and the removal of quantities of topsoil — suggest that the camp was used for research into, or the manufacture of, noxious substances.

    The common belief was that the site was a center for research into poison gas, and that the railroad line that was constructed in 1912 was for the purpose of transporting both raw materials and finished munitions.

And then, two paragraphs further down:

The departure of the army from the camp on the hill coincided with the closure of the Provost Marshal's office at New Barton. Sentinel House had been used as a regional headquarters for the military police since 1908.

At which point I felt a tap on my shoulder. Mum was standing there, her face creased with worry.

    "Matty's gone," she said.

Fifteen

I have never known anyone who has died, but at that moment, as Mum stood there surrounded by the orderly shelves of books and the quiet chat of the Reference section, I felt our world tumbling apart and the space that had been filled with chatty, excited Matty being covered with a scattering of gravel and earth.

"Where —"

"I've looked all around the library," she said. "C'mon, you'll have to help me. She's not here, Graham."

The thing was, in those few moments, I couldn't even remember what clothes she was wearing. Whether she'd worn her striped bobble-hat; whether she had on her red coat. And blue scarf? Skirt and tights? — or jeans?

But I followed Mum, who was in danger of losing control. She seemed to be having difficulty controlling her breathing, and she hadn't waited to explain what we were supposed to do. I wondered whether Matty wasn't tucked away somewhere reading a book or looking at the pictures painted by the children from a local elementary school that dominated the far wall.

When I caught up, I tugged her arm and managed to ask, "Mum, wait. What was she wearing? Was it —"

"The — her red dress — coat! Look, this, this is — impossible!"

And I thought that she was going to cry, turning away and heading for the checkout desk.

But no one in the reception area had seen a little girl with blonde hair and a red coat. And yes, it was possible that she could have slipped through the turnstile, although if she'd tried to take a library book out, the alarm would have rung. And yes, they would be happy to look out for her if we'd like to search outside.

Which was almost the end, because once through the revolving doors, we were immediately confronted by a great Amazonian flood of people, all dark clothes and exhaled breath; pushing and shoving their way toward the covered market.

"Look, Mum," I said, once more touching the sleeve of her coat. "Stay here. Don't move from here. Matty might still be in the library. And if she's slipped out, she might be trying to find her way back. You keep a watch for her. Stay here for a minute or two. I'll look in the gardens by the art gallery."

She nodded, completely defeated by the situation and as convinced as I that Matty had either wandered off or had been taken away by some sinister stranger.

I went down the steep flight of steps and turned into the crowd, away from the town center. It was like trying to swim against a strong current, my progress hindered by obstacles that might just as well have been fallen trunks — carriages, wheelchairs, shopping carts, bags stuffed with purchases.

But eventually, I made the two hundred yards beyond the Victorian front of the town art gallery and went up the stairs between the iron railings and into the library gardens.

"Hello," she said, almost immediately. "I thought you would find me."

She was standing on a stone shelf before the Roll of Honor to the Glorious Dead of the 1914–18 War. It was the list that named those killed in action.

"Oh, Matty!" I said, running up to her. "We've been so worried. We didn't know where you were."

"I'm sorry," she said. "I only just got here, Graham. I've found the *name*, Graham. The man in our house — is a soldier — there —"

And with that, her small hand reached up and touched a space after the name Weston.

I followed her pointing finger, examined the gray stone of that frozen parade. But there was no name there, not even a pattern thrown by the light.

"What, Matty?" I said. "What do you mean?"

Again she touched the place and half-turning said, "It's what he *said* — 'Whitaker, Paul Edward.' Can you see now?"

But that name wasn't there. It wasn't listed with the Harrisons and Joneses and Wainwrights and Carters. Yet she'd obviously heard something, because where else did Whitaker, Paul Edward, come from?

"Look, Matty. We've got to tell Mum you're okay. We've got to get back to the library. She's almost out of her mind with worry. Because she — we thought — someone had taken you — someone bad."

I'm not going to detail Mum's reaction. But even after everything — even after what was about to happen — she never forgot this as being one of the worst moments of her life. Almost as though she had been physically harmed in some way.

The burger place was quite a strained affair. I think Matty felt guilty but also excited. She was sad that she had wandered off without telling anyone but pleased to have discovered the identity of our visitor.

I wanted the time and the place to talk to her about it, to discover what compulsion had made her leave the library and go to the war memorial. Because the strangest thing about it was that although Matty was only five and a half and couldn't read, the place where Whitaker would have appeared in the list of dead men was exactly where her finger had touched the stone.

Once we were clear of Craybourne, the journey back to New Barton was straightforward. Mum didn't break the speed limit, but until our exit off the main road, we sped along on a surface that glistened darkly in the late afternoon sun.

As we drove along the lane to our house, John Franklin slipped off the wall that bordered our property. He shielded his eyes against the glare of our headlights and then pulled open the gates, following us and whistling a particularly off-note tune.

"He sounds happy," said Mum.

"Thought you might want to go out," he said when I emerged from the back. "Go for a ride or something?"

"We've been into Craybourne," I said.

"I called earlier, but there was no one at home. Thought I'd wait and see."

"Look, John, there's a couple of things I've got to do this afternoon, but I don't think I'm doing anything tomorrow. Maybe in the afternoon?"

"You're looking after Matty in the afternoon, Graham," said Mum, unlocking the trunk. "We've got to be at Tim Foster's at two-thirty, so I was counting on you as baby-sitter."

"Look, what about the morning?"

"Yes," he said. "About ten, then. We'll do something."

And he left as we got the shopping out of the car.

Dad had been picked up by a friend to have a look at garden ponds, so there was no one home when we got inside. Dark and silent as ever. Just the usual groans of the ancient pipework when I ran the water for the kettle and when Mum flipped the switch for the central heating.

We were in the kitchen when I heard footsteps hurrying over the gravel.

"He's back early," said Mum, looking at her watch. "I wasn't expecting him before five."

But the footsteps seemed to recede. Once heard, the crunch of gravel softened, so that whoever had been in the yard must have been moving away from the house.

I went down the corridor and opened the front door to check, but apart from the gate being slightly ajar, there was no sign of any secret lurker. The road was deserted and the streetlight glowed orange.

"Don't tell me," said Mum, holding up Matty's new dress. "Your famous ghost has been paying us a daylight visit?"

"No," I said. "There was no one there, Mum. Perhaps we were simply imagining footsteps. Or was it that aural mirage thingy that Dad was talking about?"

I'm not usually sarcastic, but I felt she was talking about something she didn't understand, had no knowledge of. I hadn't told her what Matty was up to in the library gardens, but I was convinced that whoever had been walking across our yard was not the spirit of Paul Edward Whitaker.

But we made our peace. We were both shocked by the nightmarish absence of Matty, and I think Mum was grateful that I'd been there to help during the chaos of those moments.

That afternoon at four, I found Violet Thompson's name in the phone book. On Underwood Lane, as Mr. Pyatt had said.

After I made two attempts to get the number right, a strange, withered voice came on the line: "Hello. This is New Barton seven-eight-one-five-four-two."

"Hello," I said, totally unrehearsed. "Is this Miss Thompson?"

"It is. Who is it calling, please?"

"My name's Graham Hayton, Miss Thompson. I live just down the road from you in New Barton, and I'm doing some research on the village — well, and the surrounding area."

"I see."

"I know that some years ago you wrote a pamphlet on New Barton —"

"Over twenty years ago. I'm sure that it's all pretty much out of date now."

"Well, what I was wondering, Miss Thompson, was whether I could pay you a visit over the next couple of days to ask you a few questions about the area?"

"I'm not sure I can be of much use to you — did you say your name was Graham? Well, I did all the research in the early seventies. I've still got my files and everything, my research papers, but I haven't looked at them for years. I was hoping that some publisher might be interested in my work and offer to pay the costs of printing and distribution and so forth, but no such luck, I'm afraid."

And she laughed at herself, her voice echoing around what I imagined to be a dark and empty hallway.

"But there's a copy of my pamphlet in the library at Craybourne, and they've probably gotten a lot more recent research since I was writing. Oral history has taken off lately, you know."

"I appreciate that, Miss Thompson, and I've seen your pamphlet in the library, but the thing is I've — or rather my family has recently moved into Sentinel House, and it was about the house that I wanted to question you."

There was silence — so long that I began to think I must have said something offensive. And then I wondered whether she'd accidentally cut me off.

"Miss Thompson —"

"I'm still here," she said. "You've moved into Sentinel House, you say?"

"That's right."

"Well then, I think you'll have to come over and have a chat. I'm assuming you know nothing about it?"

"Only what you wrote in your pamphlet."

"Right. Then there's something you *should* know. Could you stop by — Let me see: tomorrow I've got the ladies from the bridge club in the afternoon, and next week's not at all convenient, but you might like — Are you at school, Graham? Forgive me for asking, but your voice sounds quite young."

"Yes," I replied. "I'm fifteen. I go to James Gray."

"I see. Would you like to come to tea next Friday? At about five o'clock?"

The bus usually got me back home by 4:30, and there was nothing planned in the house that I knew of. The Americans were due on the Thursday — the 10th — so Friday sounded like it would work.

"That would be very good," I said.

"And do you eat seedcake, Graham?"

"I think so."

"Then I'll make one especially. It was Paul Whitaker's favorite."

Sixteen

And she hung up the phone.

It was like watching one of those old TV shows where something terrible or amazing threatens and the picture freezes and a voice says: "Tune in next week for the exciting conclusion." And you're left spending the following day on the bus trying to figure out how the characters are going to escape from some situation or wondering whether or not some person actually *did* commit the crime.

The creepy thing about this call was that no sooner had Matty, with all the seriousness of a five-year-old, established the identity of our visitor than Miss Thompson, with whom I had never so much as exchanged a "good morning," had as near as possible validated Matty's experience.

Supper in the kitchen was a fragmentary affair. Matty was happy to chat about the video she'd just been watching in which one of the hosts was made up as a clown. Mum listened politely and asked occasional questions, and Dad, head down with preoccupation, shoveled spaghetti and sauce into his mouth with all the relish of a machine.

I caught up with Dad just before the evening news. He was in the study, and, as he'd left the door slightly ajar, I wandered in.

He was flipping through pictures in a book about low-maintenance gardens — you know: 1,001 uses for concrete and paving stones.

"Dad," I began, as he still hadn't looked up. "What do you know about poison gas?"

He placed a hand on the page to keep his place, looked up, and said, "You mean as a weapon of war? That kind of thing?"

He had changed out of his work clothes — white shirt, jacket, and tie — and I recall he looked younger, less threatening, in jeans and a sweatshirt.

"Yes, that kind of thing."

"I'm not an expert, Graham," he replied, lines of concentration forming trenches on his forehead, "but phosgene and chlorine — gases used in the First World War — were by-products of the chemical industry. I think" — and he looked to his right at the lines of books on his shelves — "no, we used to have a paperback on the war that would have told you about gas attacks. I'm under the impression that they weren't particularly successful at the time."

"They killed people, though?"

The silence turned the room into a cavern.

He seemed to examine my face with the scrutiny you'd normally expect if you went to the doctor complaining of terminal acne.

"Look," he said, "why don't you see if there's anything on the CD encyclopedia? I'm going to be using the PC this evening, but go ahead — in the morning — that's if you still need to know about these — er — weapons of war."

Was that sarcasm? Or irony? Did he place the stress on *weapons* or not?

John turned up at 9:00 the next morning, characteristically going around to the side of the house and whacking the back door with such ferocity that Mum flung it open and said, "We're not dead, you know."

He looked up at her, startled for a second, before recovering with, "I'm sorry, Mrs. Hayton. I didn't know you'd be downstairs at this time. Thought I'd give her a belt just in case you were upstairs."

"Right. Well," she said. "You'd better come in. Graham is just finishing his breakfast."

"All right," he said without embarrassment. "Okay, Graham?"

He sat down and turned to the back of the newspaper. "Did you see that Swansea got a new manager?"

"Oh? That's fascinating." I spooned more cereal. "I need to check a couple of things on the computer. Before we go. Okay?"

"And could I have a shot at one of the games you've got?"

"Later. This will only take a minute." I dumped the bowl in the sink and led the way into the study.

The CD was one of those encyclopedias that come bundled with a new PC. It's not the most comprehensive research tool, and the index isn't so great. Look up *gas* and you'll find everything about domestic consumption but nothing about the stuff used to slaughter people. For that you need to check *chemical warfare*.

John wasn't exactly thrilled with my investigation, and after a while he went to look out the window.

Dad wasn't far off in his identification of the gases used in the First World War. The pattern was that one side would fire gas shells or release the substances from storage tanks against the enemy in nearby trenches, and then the other side would do the same.

I scrolled down.

At the top of the page titled *Gas Attacks in the First World War* was a black-and-white photograph of soldiers in a line. Each man was holding on to the shoulders of the person in front. You could tell it was winter because they were wearing heavy coats. Each person had his eyes covered with a thick, white bandage.

One young man wearing a sergeant's stripes held his face with his left hand.

From the slight blur at the foot of the picture I could tell the photographer caught these men on the move. I could hear the slow shuffle of their feet as they trudged out of the frame to some unknown destination.

The picture was simply titled *Gas Victims, Ypres, 1917*.

Looking back, I think I'd got the idea that people who were gassed died pretty quickly, like it was a quick gasp of poisoned air and the victim fell dead. Or if they didn't die, they'd spend a few days in a hospital and be all right. Perhaps with a cough or something.

But it wasn't like that. There were plenty of facts about chlorine and phosgene, but the section on mustard gas kept me fixated on the screen.

Mustard gas created great blisters on the skin and in the mouth and nose; in the windpipe and down into the lungs. It glued eyes shut with a sticky mucus and caused violent vomiting — and killed. Men were strapped to their beds because of the pain, their cries reduced to hoarse whispers as they struggled — choked — for breath.

And they died blind and alone.

It must have been the silence of the keyboard that alerted John to the fact that I'd finished and was simply sitting in Dad's chair.

"Can we go yet?" he said.

And I remember looking up at him, as though from another world, and simply saying: "Yes."

Later, as we rode our bikes past the cottages by the stream in the village, where Underwood Lane joins Craybourne Road, John shouted across, "I live down there," pointing to a row of red-brick houses. "The one that's got the Ford outside — the white one."

"Oh, right," I said.

He stopped at the intersection. "My dad has just started his own business." He laughed. "Not exactly a multinational corporation. He's using our shed as a sort of workshop. To make things."

"Make things?"

"Yes. He's good with his hands, you know. Got a lathe and all sorts of tools in the shed. Makes rocking horses for a company in London. He can make one a week."

We sat on our bikes and looked up the road. I couldn't see number 6, where Miss Thompson lived, but I had a picture of John's dad, some huge craftsman working on his rocking horses in a shed filled with wood and machinery and the smell of sawdust.

"Do you know Miss Thompson?" I asked John.

"Miss Thompson?"

"Lives at number six."

"White-haired old biddy? Sometimes walks with a walker?"

"Dunno. Never seen her, but I know she lives around here."

"Yeah," he said at last. "That's the one. Ancient. Can hardly walk. Really stooped. You know. Bent over," and he gave an impression of the angle of stoop that Miss Thompson possessed. "You'd think she was carrying cement on her back."

We spent the rest of the morning on the treed ridge above the farm. The bridle path wound along the top for about half a mile before dropping down the slope into an overgrown field that led to the road.

Where the snow had melted, the path was puddled and muddy; elsewhere just so much slush. As we hurtled along the ridge, the trees on either side breaking up the landscape like a movie reel, I wondered for the hundredth time about the way all the clues seemed to be joining together faster and faster — like Matty and the plaque to the Glorious Dead and then my conversation with Miss Thompson.

I caught up with John just before the ridge ended. He was

half-turned toward me beside the great trunk of an upturned tree.

"Toppled over one night in February," he said. "One hell of a gale. Stripped tiles off some of the houses in the village and turned this old feller on its head."

We rested our bikes on the ground and spent some minutes climbing along the bough, now horizontal, to the point where it tipped over the edge of the slope and hung out about twenty feet in the air.

"John," I said. "Why do you always come around to the side of the house? Most people go to the front door."

It was a question that I'd wondered about before but had never remembered to ask. Anyone can walk up to the front of a house, but to go through the gate and around to the side is sort of invasive. Like burglary.

"Habit," he said, walking out over the drop. He turned slowly, and then jumped. The tree quivered but didn't move. "Yeah, habit," he said, looking down. "From when we worked on the house for the Winter sisters. We always used the side entrance."

He pulled at an old twig attached to a branch.

"They were okay, but I guess they thought tradespeople should go around to the side. You know, only the gentry were allowed in through the door at the front."

"So they were —"

"Stuck up?" and he pushed the tip of his nose with a forefinger. "Probably. I just remember them as a couple of old biddies. Liked to talk. Moved like ghosts. You could be painting a baseboard and turn around to refresh your brush, and one of them would be standing over you, watching your every move. Bit creepy, if you ask me."

"Right," I said, filing away this latest bit of information about Sentinel House and its past. More disconnected fragments.

Instead of retracing our path, we took the steep slope down into the abandoned field, hurtling through the old snow and mud, splashing through concealed pools and skidding on ice. We stopped by a stile that was partly hidden by the surrounding hawthorn.

Later, as we approached Underwood Lane, John said, "Come and have a look at the workshop. The old man's just finished one of the horses. Hasn't started to paint it yet. You'll be amazed." And again he laughed.

The house was on the corner, on the right. The Ford was still there. We went through the metal gate and up the concrete path to the right of the lawn.

"Here," he said. "Lean your bike against the fence. It'll be all right. Not many thieves around here."

The shed was a building at the back, running the full width of the garden. The long window was screened with a Venetian blind, and as we approached I could hear someone whistling.

There was something familiar about it that I wasn't able to put my finger on, but when John opened the door and I'd absorbed the single bulb, the unpainted rocking horse, and the rack of tools, I found myself face-to-face with the twisted smile of Mr. David Thomas.

"Hi," said John. "This is Graham."

Seventeen

TD/MH: 5/17/99

MH   We went down. We were . . . alone. Locked in. It
was dark. There was a window. It was gray. There
were cobwebs. I thought of spiders crawling — in
the dark. We could — we could hear people's feet
above. In the room above. There were other sounds.
We listened. [pause] When, when we opened the
window — it didn't want — it was hard to open the
window. We couldn't get out. There were bars. There
was no other way. We were left. In the dark with
loud footsteps.

Eighteen

"Ah, Graham," he said, wiping his hands on his apron. "Good to see you. Been out for a ride, I see."

I wasn't in the mood for a chat, so I could hardly blurt out anything sensible. I nodded in an idiot kind of way.

"Bit of a surprise, is it?" he went on, John going over to the bench at the far side to pick up a chisel.

"I'm John's stepdad, you see. I've been with his mam for so long that we're like one cuddly family these days. We all live together, work together and" — he laughed — "play together."

He smiled, and the strings on his face clenched into a kind of grimace.

"You'll be pleased to know I've got the old modem up and running. Goes like a rocket now. Next step: the Internet! But enough of that. What do you think of my newfound hobby? If you were a bit smaller, I'd let this little fellow take you for a ride," he said, and he patted the wooden flank of the horse. It moved backward under his touch as if slowly coming to life.

"'Course I'd be nothing without my trusty helper and his

spray gun," he added, and he gestured toward John, who was tapping his chisel into a block of wood clenched in a vise.

"I didn't know you ran your own business," I was able to say at last, while looking around through the particles of sawdust at the discarded tools on the bench, the sets of goggles and face masks on the wall, the tattered seaside calendar, and the picture of some guy with a beard, black hair, and stubby cigar.

"Well, bit early to say *business* yet," he said. "But we live and hope. And if you'll now excuse me — John — I need to get this chap on his way before five this afternoon." He pulled his face mask down and reached for the electric sander.

Outside there was a slight gauze of rain in the air, and the sky was several layers of gray.

"You never told me he was your father," I said. "He's been in our house, you know."

"I know," said John. "I couldn't see the point. And it was sort of " — and he paused to get the word right — "awkward. You know: saying he's my dad, but he's not my dad, and we have different names and everything. I mean, does it matter?"

I thought about this as my bike ticked slowly down Underwood Lane and past the silent number 6. It was all so strange. Spending time with John and helping his stepdad, but neither of them acknowledging the existence of the other.

I explained my discovery to Mum on my return. She was in a kitchen soft with steam and warmth, carefully paring a bowl of brussels sprouts. All she said, having turned off the radio, was, "I expect he was a bit embarrassed. You know, Mr. Thomas and John's mum might simply be living together. And there's all that business of different names to explain away. No," she said finally, "I don't really find it that odd. You know," she added, and she turned toward me, smiling in a knowing kind of way, "people get worried about all sorts of silly things."

Well, quite frankly, I couldn't see what she was getting at, so after checking the sports page in the paper, I joined Dad in the study.

I can't really say why I needed more discussion with the resident arms merchant, particularly since he was so preoccupied with selling his deadly know-how to the Americans, but I think I wanted in some way to discuss with him what I'd found on the CD. It seemed that the use of gas was almost playground stuff: first one side would attack the opposition — killing thousands — and then the other side would do the same. Wasn't this really all there was to it? Grown men with dangerous toys.

And I think also — and maybe I write this because of what later happened — there was somewhere knocking around in my head my idea of the old Dad. He wasn't ever like the father in that Roald Dahl movie *Danny, the Champion of the World,* but before he came a creature of Spere Electronics, and when I was small, he seemed to have more time.

He and Mum had this agreement that he would read the bedtime story twice a week. And at first he would turn up in my bedroom in the old house and pick up whatever was on top of the pile of books, and he would do his best to inject life into the reading.

But I don't think his heart was ever in the project. I think fiction, even the picture-book variety, bored him stupid, so that one evening, when the light was fading and my bedside lamp glowed orange, he came in and sat on the bed and said something like, "Would you like me to tell you a story tonight? Not from a book or anything, but just like — uh — talking to you?"

And I said something like, "What would the story be about?"

And he said, "About an amazing man who changed the world."

And I said, "Let's go!"

And that's when Isambard Kingdom Brunel entered my life. Quite frankly, with a name like that and the way Dad told the story over the next few weeks, I thought he was making it all up and that Brunel was more or less a figure like the Big Friendly Giant, particularly because he was engaged in such amazing stuff, like getting washed out of tunnels under a river, inventing an amazing new form of transportation, and throwing a bridge over a two-hundred-foot gorge. But when we all went to Bristol, and we saw the slender beauty of the Clifton bridge with Brunel's name engraved on the uprights, it was like finding out that there was a Santa Claus.

There is even a picture of Brunel in Dad's study, on the bulletin board behind his desk: a small man in a top hat chewing on a cigar and completely overshadowed by this huge pile of massive chains that were being used to launch Brunel's ship, the *Great Eastern*.

Anyway, this gives you a bit of the context as I wandered down the corridor that morning to chat with Dad. I stuck my head around the door, trying to switch on my Mr. Affable expression, but he didn't even look up from the monitor.

"I'm a bit busy at the moment. I should be done soon."

I'd like to write here that I went down later and we had a good old father-and-son talk. But this isn't a cozy soap opera. And no, it didn't happen.

Nineteen

Mum and Dad were going over to visit their friends that afternoon. The Fosters lived on the other side of Craybourne, and Mum and Dad were due at 2:30, so they were ready and by the front door a little after ten of two.

"Right," said Mum. "The number is by the phone if you need to call. There are cookies in the cabinet and some banana cake in the tin. We'll be back by —" she looked at Dad, who was standing with his hands stuffed into his overcoat pockets.

"Six?" he suggested.

"We'll be back between six and half-past. Okay?"

And they went out, through the door and into the overcast yard. It was December 6.

Matty and I hadn't spent much time alone together, so it was slightly odd, just the two of us in that large house. She didn't seem concerned that Mum and Dad had gone out, and we both settled down in front of the TV. This wasn't my number-one Sunday activity, but I thought it would be a friendly thing to do.

The choices weren't terrific when it came down to it, and after watching *Cartoon Cavalcade*, we tuned in to a movie and watched eighteenth-century pirates make their way across a pile of rocks on some palm-fringed coast. They were following a map that one of them was clutching, and eventually they discovered the mouth of a sea cave. This was where the buried treasure was supposed to be. Well, after about five seconds of watching them dig, Matty tugged at my sleeve.

"Graham," she said, "have you been in the cellar?"

"Yeah — once in a while. It's not very interesting, you know. Just old boxes and Dad's collection of bottles."

"Well, could we have a look in a minute?"

I couldn't really see the attraction, quite frankly, but if that was her heart's desire, let's do it, I thought.

"Sure," I said, and I got up. "We'll have a look now."

I should explain that the cellar extends for about half the floor area of the house. The entrance is via a door in the paneled wall under the stairs.

The room isn't enormous or anything, but it is slightly creepy, because since the light switch is concealed on one of the beams that supports the first floor, unless you take some light with you, you're wandering in the dark until you find it.

That day I didn't know where a spare flashlight was, but I recalled that the basement window gave some light, so we went down the steps, turned to the right under the old gas pipes, and found ourselves in a space filled with shadows, old boxes, and the dark stain of mildew that spread across the floor and up the wall.

"It smells funny," said Matty, holding my hand.

"Yeah — it's just the damp. These bricks" — and I pointed — "rest on the earth. Now let me just see —" and I started to feel the sides of the overhead beams for the hidden switch.

"Ssshhh!" she said suddenly, clutching my sweater. "What was that noise?"

Neither of us moved. Her fear seemed to infect the room, and I felt the hairs bristle on the back of my neck.

At first, in the twilight, I couldn't make anything out. The house seemed unusually silent, but then, quite clearly and quite distinctly, came the first footfall of someone walking above. He wasn't making a lot of noise, but the clear tap of a tread on the kitchen tiles came down to us.

Matty seemed to be shivering, leaning against me for comfort. Neither of us spoke. Both of us knew that the cellar door was pulled open and completely visible to anyone walking through the house.

And then the sound stopped, as if someone was up there listening — like one of those house spiders you sometimes see in the evening, halfway out of the dark, front leg poised, waiting. That silence, as we strained to hear, was almost worse than the first tread, and it got to the point when I thought we'd imagined something, that it was really just the house giving one of its periodic groans. But we hadn't, because the sound of a stranger slowly crossing the floor came down to us, and the footsteps didn't stop.

Tap-tap-tap, slowly and steadily, traveling to where we stood.

I think it was instinct for survival more than anything else that made us move toward the wall and away from the center of the room at the precise moment that a long shadow began to flow down the stairs, dripping down step by step until we knew that the intruder was standing at the opening, looking down.

The figure waited and waited. Listening.

I don't think breath passed my lips in thirty seconds. The world seemed to have shrunk to just me and a terrified child trying to conceal ourselves in the half-dark.

And then — well — the black stain abruptly flowed back up the stairs, and the cellar door banged shut. The key turned, and we were locked in.

At that point, her body shaken by a series of great shudders, Matty started to cry. Not loudly, but like a car starting on a cold day with a few great heaves of effort, and then the tears fell with the sudden release of tension. I hunkered down beside her. I whispered, "It's okay Matty. We're all right."

All the time listening for sounds up above.

I think she was too wise to the situation to completely give in to her feelings, and I think she also realized that whoever had entered our house might also return to the cellar — might also come down that flight of steps and find us there.

And so we stood and listened, trying to make out the tremor of human activity in the rooms above.

The person was in the study.

There was absolutely no doubt about that. Over to the right, I heard the electronic spring of the monitor being turned on and then the squeak of someone sitting down in the swivel chair.

I put my finger to my lips and crossed the room to the window. It was filthy with dust and cobwebs and neglect. The frame was beginning to rot, and the fastener in the middle was difficult to turn. And when I did finally ease back the clasp, the window seemed cemented together, locked as if both edges had been liberally slathered with glue.

I paused and looked up at the sky glimpsed through the metal grid that shut us off from the outside world and then turned to Matty and shook my head. There was no point in opening the window if we couldn't get through the bars to the garden above.

We listened to the house for a few moments, but it was completely silent. No sound from the study. No footsteps. I waited for a minute longer and then went over to the steps, carefully treading through the minefield of old boxes.

I could see a strip of light from the hall shining in at the foot of the door, but once I was at the top, the handle firmly grasped, it was obvious we weren't going to escape that way.

Matty hadn't moved when I got back. She was standing still in the middle of the cellar and looking up at the ceiling.

It was at this moment that I saw the white plastic of the switch. There didn't seem to be any point in not giving ourselves some light, particularly as the intruder must know that we were there.

And yet when, moments later, the area was flooded by the single bulb, I think we both felt horribly exposed. The shadows gave the illusion of security, but now there was no place to run.

"I don't like this," said Matty. "He might see us. It's too much light."

And I gave in to her feelings, partly, I must admit, on account of my own uneasiness at our situation. And so, for twenty minutes, we sat in semidarkness on wooden boxes and waited for the intruder to go.

Eventually, of course, he did.

Matty and I both looked up at the same time when we heard the snap of a wall switch being turned off. And then the muffled sound of feet over the carpet. To the door, then down the corridor, almost directly overhead, to the cellar entrance.

For one brief moment, he stopped there, waiting not fifteen yards from where we sat, and then moved on, through the kitchen. Then silence. No sound of a gravel tread. He must have disappeared over the back wall into the cow field.

I flipped the light switch on.

"Are you all right?" I said.

"Yes, I think so," she replied, her face smudged with dirt.

"I think we'll be safe now. Although it might get a bit chilly waiting for Mum and Dad."

Two minutes later, Matty got up from her box and, as if drawn there, went over to the wall next to the old coal chute. She brushed away some dirt and then turned and said, "Come and see, Graham. Look."

And there, quite faint but cut into the dark brick, were the letters PEW.

I stared at them for a moment, seeing only the uneven spacing and shape of the lines. Then something nudged my memory. "Paul Edward Whitaker," I said.

Twenty

The marks were low down, about four inches from the ground. And after the *W* could be made out one of those government arrows that prisoners once wore on their uniforms in old times.

"The arrow points down," said Matty, outlining the mark with her forefinger. "Perhaps there's something buried there."

And I had a flash of the TV pirates shoveling Hollywood sand to reach their treasure chest.

"No, no, Matty. That's a mark that indicates the property of the government. They used to stamp all sorts of stuff with it, including the clothes worn by convicts. I think it shows that PEW was a prisoner here."

"And that was why he was sad?"

"I expect so," I replied, and I went back to my box.

She wandered around the room for several minutes, occasionally touching the walls and sometimes bending down to peer into the dark of the corners.

"Do you think we could lift some of the bricks — over

there — where the arrow points?" she said after completing several circuits. "Please."

The floor of the cellar was completely bricked over, and as far as I could see, the builders hadn't used any mortar. That explained the damp of the area, and it probably wouldn't be too hard to move a brick or two if you were enthusiastic about seeing what was underneath.

The problem was, they were tightly packed together and to lift one would require an implement the width of a knife to slide down between the two surfaces and exert some force.

I explained this to Matty, and the pair of us looked through the boxes scattered across the floor in the hope that an abandoned picnic hamper packed with cutlery might materialize.

It was while we were rifling through bottles and jam jars and all the other dusty paraphernalia that the phone began to ring upstairs in the hall.

We both stopped and waited. It went on and on and on. And then stopped.

"Probably someone for Dad," I said. He received most of the telecommunications traffic in the house. But then the ringing started again. And, as before, continued for the best part of two minutes. There seemed to be an urgency to the call, as if the caller had expected someone to lift the receiver and was checking in case he'd misdialed.

"It could be Mummy," said Matty. "Phoning to see that we're okay."

"Yeah," I said. "And if it is them, they'll call again. I bet you."

It was already four, and already the sky outside through the window was three-quarters night, and this made the room darker. The light was no better than 60 watts, and it threw great shadows across the floor and walls.

"What about this?" said Matty suddenly.

It was an old steel ruler. I thought it was a fraction too thick, but we had nothing better to work with, so I said, "Okay. Let's give it a try."

Trying to slide that piece of metal between bricks that had been jammed together for decades was difficult, and it took me several frustrating attempts before I realized that I might have better luck if I pushed the ruler down the side that had contact with the wall.

After five minutes of this I went back and sat on the box.

"I think we're getting somewhere, Matty, but this could be a long job." At which point, the phone in the hall started to give out its call again.

"What did I tell you?" I said. "They'll realize something's wrong, and they'll be on their way."

Or so we hoped.

The major breakthrough came when Matty saw movement as I exerted maximum pressure, and, eventually, we were able to insert the metal along one of the ends. This opened up a crack about a tenth of a millimeter wide.

When we finally lifted the brick clear, we both bent over the dark gap to see if our treasure was there waiting to be discovered. But there was only densely packed earth marked with the imprint of the Portsmouth Brick Company.

After all that work — it was past 4:30 by this time — all we had retrieved was a lump of baked clay.

Then Matty touched the cold surface of the earth with her fingers and delicately, slowly, scraped away a thin coating of dirt to uncover the shape of a heavily rusted metal box, two-thirds the length of the brick we had just removed.

She looked up at me.

"I was right, wasn't I?" she said, her mouth spreading into a jaw-breaking grin. "We have discovered treasure."

Twenty-one

I took out another brick to give us room for maneuvering and then, very carefully, aware of its age, brought out the box.

Originally it had been painted. Through the thick rust we could see traces of dark blue. In the bottom left-hand corner could be read *16 oz.,* and I thought it might be a tobacco tin, the kind used by pipe smokers.

"Let's see what's inside," said Matty. "Come on, Graham, open it!"

We moved our seats to the middle of the cellar, underneath the lightbulb, and I handed the box to Matty.

"Go on," I said. "This is your discovery. You open it."

The metal was flaky with decay, but after a few seconds, she inched back the lid and we both saw what looked like a wad of yellow, greasy paper.

I was all set to be disappointed, prepared to accept that the contents had been damaged, but Matty delicately touched the old surface and, balancing the box on her knees, gently brought out a package that I now know had been hidden eight decades before.

We were both silent, in that strange light, in that cold place, as she carefully pulled back the paper and revealed a small book, a pocket watch, a discolored cigarette case, and three coins.

"These were put here by Paul Whitaker," she said. "I think he was kept prisoner. He put his best things in this box — for someone to find."

The cigarette case was densely worked with curls and curves, and in an oval on the front, the letters *PEW* were joined together.

"Well, there's his initials, Matty," I said, and I pointed to the patterning.

She was busy looking through the pages of the small book.

It was a pocket-size version of *The Pilgrim's Progress* by John Bunyan, and we could see from the wear and tear that it had been carefully read. Inside the front cover and facing the title page, a J. B. Roberts, vicar, had written:

TO PAUL WHITAKER FOR PERSEVERANCE, PUNCTUALITY,

AND ATTENDANCE AT CRAYBOURNE ELEMENTARY SCHOOL

JULY 1912

The watch seemed to be made from steel, because the metal back plate was rusted and stained. We could make out the serial number 30350W and the arrow that made it government property. The winder no longer turned, and the time was forever fixed at eleven minutes after five.

Matty was quite interested in the coins — two farthings and an old penny — and I explained the old money system as well as I was able.

After that, we sat close together on our wooden perches, and I read from the old book the long journey of Christian in his wilderness. Trying to put out of my mind the question of why anyone might need to hide such a strange assortment of articles in the first place.

It was quite dark outside when we heard the sound of a car approaching and then saw the sweep of headlights and heard the crunch of tires moving over gravel.

"There aren't any lights on," I heard Mum say. "I'm worried, Brian."

Their footsteps came closer. And then Dad spoke.

"There's a light on in the cellar. Look!"

We were both at the window, staring up through the grille. I saw Dad's face looking down and shouted out, "We're down here. We're okay. We're locked in!"

We were released twenty seconds later. It was just after half past five, and we'd been down there over three hours.

"Someone came into the house. They locked us in the cellar," said Matty. "We were very frightened," and for a moment, as she relived the experience, I thought that she might start crying.

"What happened, Graham?" asked Dad, looking anxious.

And I explained:

"Well, we spent a while watching TV, and then Matty said

she'd like to take a look in the cellar. I didn't see a problem with that, so we went down. I was looking for the light switch because I didn't take a flashlight with me, when Matty heard someone moving around in the house."

"He was in the kitchen," she said. "We heard his feet on the floor. He came toward the cellar. I thought he was going to come down the steps. I thought he was going to get us —" and she started to cry. The huge relief that the ordeal had ended, that we were safe and that life could continue on its course, was overwhelming. And I have to confess I, too, felt the first surges of emotion since we'd been locked in.

Dad looked around the kitchen, went through into the laundry, and checked the back door. He turned the handle and went and looked at the side window.

"Well, there's no sign of a break-in. I'll just call the police — might as well get them on the scene."

When he'd gone, Mum asked, "How long was this person in the house? Do you know where he went? Did you get any idea who he might be?"

"We never saw the person. I think there was only one. He was here for about twenty minutes. He spent the time in the study. We heard the computer being used — you know, the sound of the monitor being switched on and the chair being sat on."

"But we found an old box, Mummy — in the cellar," said Matty, "and it had coins and a book and other things."

But Mum seemed distracted by what I'd told her, and when she repeated the information to Dad, he went straight back into the study to check for signs of theft.

Police Sergeant Masters was on the scene half an hour later.

He was a tall man with silver hair and bushy eyebrows. He sat at the kitchen table with a mug of tea and listened while I explained what had happened, making notes and occasionally asking questions. When I'd finished, he summarized my version of events.

And then, turning to Mum and Dad, he said, "Well, Mr. and Mrs. Hayton, to put it mildly, we haven't got a lot to go on. You've got someone who lets himself into the house, locks the children in the cellar, spends twenty minutes or so in the study, probably using the computer, and then leaves the building.

"No one saw him arrive or depart. The door at the rear of the house is secure, and all of the windows are locked. There is no sign of a break-in, and you say nothing has been taken. Even if we were to lay our hands on the person who did this thing, he could simply turn around and say, 'What crime?'

"Is there anything on the computer that might attract a villain into the house? — you know, I don't want to pry, but is there something that someone might wish to steal from you or at least look at?"

"Well, no," said Dad, straight-faced. "There's nothing on the hard disk to tempt anyone, and the floppies are locked away in the office at work."

"There are no files or folders or bits of paper or anything like that lying around?"

"No. I've got to be careful because of the work I do. The study is clean."

"Well, if anything does occur to you, here's my card and number. Give me a call."

And with that, he placed a broad rubber band around his notebook, drained the last dregs of tea from his mug, and disappeared into the night.

Twenty-two

On frosty Sundays you can hear the church bells from Brenton Underwood quite clearly. They start at about 10:30 and persist until 11:00. I sometimes notice their cascades of sound while lying on my back, reconciled to the thought of no further sleep.

I mention this because I've recently been asked: "Where did you put the experience of Paul Whitaker?"

That means, I think, how did I cope with the idea of living in a haunted house without having religion to fall back on?

We weren't Christians or Buddhists or Muslims or anything, so the matter of the afterlife never really came up. Matty still had faith in Father Christmas, but that's different, I suppose. And for that matter, where did Matty *put* the experience?

Sometimes she was very unhappy — I think more because of the sadness of the young man who spoke to her. And I sometimes got the feeling that she just regarded him as another part of her hugely inventive imagination, and that she and I were in some way involved in an elaborate game.

Up until the moment I spoke to Violet Thompson, I tried not to allow the idea of the dead speaking to the living to intrude too much into my life. I kind of tricked myself that there were rational explanations for everything and that the only person who had regular contact with Paul Whitaker was a five-year-old.

My conversation with Violet Thompson took a hammer to that view.

Anyway, two restless nights after the cellar experience — and this would be December 8 — I found myself back at school going through the door of room 37 in search of Mr. Pyatt.

He was sorting through videos when I arrived, looking for "something suitable to entertain the eighth-graders," but at long last, and before sunset, he sat behind his desk, pushed his lunch box away, and said, "Tell me where we are."

And then, after the summary, he scratched his ear as if unsure that he'd heard correctly and came back with: "And what conclusion do you come to?," his fingers lightly touching the rusted box I'd brought from home.

I think that at that moment I wanted someone else to take some responsibility; to make ordinary sense out of an extraordinary experience.

"I was hoping you might tell me, Mr. Pyatt," I said.

He opened the lid and placed the book, cigarette box, watch, and coins on the table. And then: "It would seem, Graham, that if a soldier named Paul Whitaker was staying at Sentinel House in the first war, he was either a member of the military police — a redcap — or —"

"He had been arrested?"

"Exactly. And" — pointing to the stuff on his table — "if it was the latter, if he was some kind of prisoner there, why would he bury his personal possessions in the house? What are we looking at that was so important to him?"

At that point he picked up Bunyan's book and carefully flipped through the pages.

"Hmmm, various bits underlined and a couple of marginal comments, but hardly the clue we're looking for. Obviously a Christian, but you'd hardly get locked up for that, unless . . . What I was thinking — and this may be a bit of a long shot, Graham: Was Paul Whitaker someone who went through a great change in his way of thinking? Like he found belief — and in some way this got him into trouble? Like — maybe — the work he was being forced to do was suddenly against his principles? Something he couldn't cope with?"

He held the book by its covers and gently pushed them back to expose the gap between the pages and the spine.

"Ah!" he said. "What have we here?" And he reached into his desk drawer, rummaged for a moment, and then produced a pair of tweezers — the kind Mum used to pluck her eyebrows.

He held the book open horizontally and slowly extracted a length of paper.

"I think *this* is why he hid the box. This is the great secret that needed to be kept from prying eyes."

There was a single sheet, unlined and torn roughly along one side. It was covered in closely written pencil script.

Mr. Pyatt smoothed it out gently across his desk and turning to me said, "Shall I read it out, Graham?"

I nodded, and after adjusting his glasses, he began:

11th February 1918

I do not know at which time or place my life shall end, but I know that as God is my guide I have done my duty to my conscience and I dedicate this testament to brothers unknown.

I pledge that everything revealed in these lines was witnessed by myself, Paul Edward Whitaker, Private, Wiltshire Regiment, and that in consequence of my indiscretion it is likely that I shall receive stern punishment.

I was placed under close arrest by comrades of the Provost Marshal's office on the 8th January 1918 and charged with treason.

On the 21st I was defendant in a court-martial at Sentinel House, New Barton. It was said that I did write a letter to The Times *newspaper in London, saying that the work being carried out at New Barton camp was concerned with the making of poisonous gas, and that prisoners in the custody of the Provost Marshal's office were used in experiments to test the results of the substances being manufactured.*

On the advice of Captain King, I admitted the charge as stated in the indictment, but I pleaded for my good conduct and service record to be taken into account when sentence was being considered.

I own that I have no great hopes for mercy, and Captain King advised that I should make my peace with God in the expectation of an absolute sanction.

During frontline duty near Arras, I saw how my comrades, their eyes and lips blistered and red, twisted in pain on the dirty ground. How, in the great clouds of poison gas, they spewed blood and choked to their deaths.

My work as clerk at New Barton did not concern me in the making of any ordnance or arranging its use, but to be aware of the suffering of fellow creatures, to be a helpmate in the cause of death, is an abomination I could endure no longer and I gave witness to what I knew.

That my endeavor was fruitless, I can now acknowledge. But if I am to receive a capital sentence, I here entrust these words to the safety of the good earth, and hope that in future, peaceful times, a reader might find lack of regard for narrow patriotism a virtue rather than a treasonous vice.

Paul Whitaker, Private

Mr. Pyatt read the words slowly, sometimes halting when a crease in the paper or the faded hand made understanding difficult. When he had finished, we sat in silence.

I looked across the room and out over the playing field to the houses on the estate. There was a black-headed gull on sentry duty on top of one of the football posts, and below, speckling the green, half a dozen others mingled with a flock of starlings.

I thought back to the morning when John and I had crawled through the wire and wandered across the rain-swept desolation of the old camp by Wilson's Wood. The very place where gas experiments had been carried out on British prisoners. And where one young man broke ranks and took their part.

I thought, too, of the letters written in the condensation of my window, the word *Gas* bleeding away on the glass.

"An extraordinary story," said Mr. Pyatt eventually. "I don't suppose Miss Thompson got any of that from the Ministry of Defense."

"What do you think happened to him?" I said.

Mr. Pyatt paused, touching the paper lightly with his forefinger. "I don't know, Graham. He was put on trial for his life, and he confessed to a very serious offense. He would have been a lucky man to have survived. I think you'll have to wait until you see Miss Thompson on Friday. I have a hunch that she might hold a vital piece of the puzzle."

Twenty-three

It's still difficult to comprehend the twenty-four hours surrounding that next Thursday.

When I go through the sequence, I remember that December 10 was overcast and gray from start to finish. That we had a cross-country run in the afternoon and that I discovered an uneaten cheese sandwich in my bag on the way home.

I remember eating it while watching the rain, like beads of sweat, stream against the windows of the bus.

Of course it was the day of the American visitors and the eve of Dad's great sales presentation. Dad had been gone an hour by the time I sat down to breakfast that morning, and Matty had spent the meal stirring great puddles of syrup into her porridge before deciding she didn't want it after all.

The Americans were due at 8:30, and although the original idea was that I would take part in the meal, Dad thought it would be easier on my social skills, and give the occasion greater focus, if I ate at the conventional hour of 5:30, got introduced to the "dudes from across the pond," and then spent some time in my room. Like the rest of the evening.

I wasn't devastated by the change of plans, although it did seem crazy to have to get dressed in my new jacket and trousers just for a few moments of touching base.

Mum wasn't particularly bothered by the prospect of VIPs. Once she'd worked out that the evening might have an Italian flavor, she started working through pasta recipes in her various cookbooks. During that week, the break-in forgotten, she'd suddenly interrupt stuff we were doing — homework or computer programming; watching TV or eating supper — and say, "What do you think of this? Do you think it might be a bit too much as a first course?"

And she'd explain what the dish involved and how it contrasted to the projected main course and so on and so forth.

My suggestion: "Mum, why don't you do a couple of pizzas and some salad with that purple-colored lettuce? Everyone likes pizza. Have a few bottles of wine to warm the conversation. That'll be great."

All this met with five seconds of *silenzio*. And then the big freeze-out: "No, no, Graham. You simply don't understand. This is an important occasion for your father — well, for all of us — and we want it to be a great success."

So maybe my earlier observation about Mum being unconcerned was way off base. Looking back over it now, I guess that whole week was filled with tension. What with the Americans arriving and the sales presentation and the fact that the locks on the doors front and back were being replaced and a security light installed in the garden. Plus the fact that I woke up two nights in a row convinced there was something wrong in the house.

On that Thursday, and for the last time, I sat in Dad's bathroom and chatted to him while he shaved. I listened to the sound of the blade scraping over his chin and the occasional splash of water, trying to find a way to open a conversation.

"Odd, really, that someone who works in high tech should use old technology to shave with."

He looked down at me for a second, perhaps wondering whether I was going to ask him for a loan.

"Well, you can't beat it, can you?" he said and then resumed scraping. "Learned this at my father's knee. Something comforting about it." He splashed the razor into the water. "It's quality thinking time, you know!"

"I know that the sales thing you're involved in is important for the company and everything, but doesn't it bother you that you might be sort of — well — helping in some war effort that might lead —"

"— to innocent lives being lost? Arms sales overseas? That kind of thing? Excuse me one second," he said, and he bent over the sink to splash water over his cheeks.

"Sure I do. Yes!" He reached down and picked up a towel. "But that kind of thinking goes nowhere. If it wasn't me, it would be someone else. But more to the point, the selling of arms is quite well controlled nowadays, you know. Don't worry about it!"

He rinsed his hands under the faucet, ruffled my hair, and pushed past me into the future.

*　　*　　*

The Americans rolled up at twenty to nine in one of those large cross country-style vehicles — you know, high axle and large treads.

They were named Jeff and Tom. Jeff was shiny bald with large, light-reflecting teeth, and Tom was tall and thin, with a scraggly mustache and said "Howdy" as if he'd walked in off the streets of Abilene.

Although I never got the chance to check back with Mum — because everything kind of fell apart after that — I remember feeling how big and confident and, well, sort of exotic they were. Like they'd stepped out of the frame of some TV show. And I suppose that's because most people's experience of Americans is through movies and the news. They were like huge tropical butterflies that had just flown in from the coast.

I did my best to remain inconspicuous so that I could hang around and stare, but at ten past nine Mum said that the meal was only five minutes away, so I said good night and shuffled off to flip through a book on UFOs.

From what I heard from my room, that part of the evening went well. Dad was enthusing about some software he'd just encountered; the Americans, particularly Tom, were fascinated by British place-names.

"And how do you pronounce *Sal-is-bury?*"

And Mum was busy with the cannelloni in the kitchen.

Later Dad gave the visitors a preview of the video on the StarRaider. The twin engines boomed and roared up the stairs, gunning and twisting in a tight turn past the bookshelf before screaming out low over the carpet.

After the air display, I discarded the text on aliens and, as I recall, crashed into sleep listening to an old Frank Zappa album filched from the music room at school. I woke up to something entirely different.

At first I had that moment of disorientation like when you're staying in someone else's place and you open your eyes and wonder where you are. It was quite dark in the room — a low cloud base totally cut off any lurking rays from the moon — and the house seemed quiet.

But something wasn't right — as if the bed were at the wrong angle or a door were banging. I felt cold, and the air was thick with expectation. And then, in the distance, but coming closer, the tramp-tramp of marching feet. Hundreds of men pounding the ground.

I had in mind Dad's earlier observation about an aural mirage — sound waves carried over great distances on clear nights. But this wasn't like that. The noise got closer, seemed to hang in the air and fade momentarily, and then would rush on again. Coming toward us like the incoming tide pushing up a beach.

Closer and closer.

Looking back, it was hypnotic in a way, like listening to a steam engine heading in from a great distance. The dense weight of hundreds of boots crashing in unison; the pounding pistons of some great machine.

But soon, noise filled the room, filled the house. And everything seemed to be shaking. I could hear stuff on my shelves — a model of the *QE II,* a scattering of fossils from a field trip — start to vibrate, like the ground beneath us was beginning to shift and turn.

There was a cry from along the corridor. There was a crash from downstairs, and then the whole parade was on us, hammering through the house; bursting through the walls and doors like the rush of the sea smashing sand castles built by a child.

There were lights on in the corridor and a cascade of noise below — breaking wood and wrenching metal. A great screaming wash of sound.

And then, as I heard footsteps on the stairs, there was silence. Like one second there's a force-nine gale breaking up the sea, and the next the water is as still as a millpond. Like the spasm of grief you get from children followed by the abrupt quiet once a source of comfort has been found.

Matty was crying; and Dad's voice came from somewhere down below: "This is unbelievable. Kate, you'd better come and have a look."

Clear through the house, through the study, through the living room, a path had been driven. The computer table was in two pieces, upended like a torpedoed ship, and the monitor was on its side, a massive crack splintering the glass.

Books and files littered the floor, and a pool of black ink glistened on the carpet.

The smash-up in the living room — the coffee table thrown against one of the walls, both armchairs upended, yesterday's vase of flowers shattered across the hearth, a jagged line cracking the paper on the far wall — mirrored the wreckage in the study.

In both rooms the pattern was clear: everything had been driven to one side. The walls were intact, but a path had broken through the house as clearly as a troop of soldiers blazing a trail in the Burmese jungle.

Dad lifted the phone in the hall, had just got to the second 9 in the sequence, when the sound of an approaching car made him pause. We saw the headlights of a vehicle entering our drive, and then the front doorbell started to ring.

It was the police.

"Mr. Hayton?" asked the first officer, and I noticed a second car waiting in the road outside.

"Yes," said Dad, obviously perplexed.

"We'd like you to get dressed and accompany us to the Craybourne police station. I'm arresting you for disclosing information classified under Section 2 of the 1989 Official Secrets Act."

Twenty-four

Friday started clear and cold and stayed that way.

My hands felt the chill as I pedaled down the road into New Barton, toward Underwood Lane.

It was already eleven, but no one was around, and only the smoke from one of the cottages gave the impression of life. Everything else was listless and still.

The police had arrived at 2:30. The officers glanced at the wreckage on the first floor and then passed an instruction to a colleague back at Craybourne.

But the second group didn't appear until 4:00 and after inspecting the outside of the house and asking obvious questions went away as puzzled as the rest of us. A fingerprint check was to be made during normal working hours.

I stopped the bike by the stream and watched the water slip past a piece of rotting chestnut. It had been there since October, since some kids had pelted the tree to give up its clutch of conkers. The leaves on the branch were long gone, and as the water flowed past, so the wood moved gently in the current.

We weren't able to sort out the confusion in the living room and study. The police were very clear that both areas were to be subject to further investigation by the Special Branch. Each door was locked and sealed, a procedure that added a further layer of nightmare, as if we were being gradually evicted from our own home.

At half past nine, Mum called the Craybourne station. There was a long delay while she was transferred from department to department before: "I see. And we can't come over and visit him?"

"He's being held for questioning," she said when she replaced the handset. There were dark smudges beneath her eyes; a strand of hair had come undone and hung across her face.

"They won't let me visit him. Arthur Bellamy, our lawyer, has been there to find out what's going on."

We sat in the kitchen and drank coffee. I think we were both hoping that the front door would suddenly open, Dad would walk in, and everything would carry on as before. Dad would say something like: "Incredible mistake. Thought I was someone else. Now, is that coffee I smell?"

But of course, it wasn't like that. When Bellamy called, it was to relay the coarse facts of the case. I sat at the top of the stairs with Matty, trying to make sense of the conversation:

"But that's plainly ridiculous. Have they considered his record with Spere? . . . I know, Mr. Bellamy — . . . Yes, but why would he want to do that? Even I can see — . . . So we'll be able to visit him this afternoon? This evening? For heaven's sake! This *is* ridiculous!"

She was standing in the kitchen looking out over the garden

when we went down. Her voice was tired and flat. "Mr. Bellamy says that the operating details of the StarRaider aircraft — the software Dad was working on for Spere — have been published on the Internet. The American company that wanted the technology has discovered this and has broken off negotiations."

She paused, as if trying to comprehend what she'd just said.

"Because of the nature of the work Dad was engaged in, any publication of this information is strictly against the Official Secrets Act. Dad signed the act when he went to work for Spere, so he was aware of his obligations —"

"But Dad wouldn't have —" I began.

"No. He's denied all knowledge of what has happened, but the police say that they have traced back from the Web site, and all paths lead to this door. They say there's absolutely no doubt that the source of the information — how it got on the Internet — is our number."

The white Ford was parked outside John's house, and I dutifully propped my bike against the fence.

Looking back from this distance, I think I went there simply because I couldn't stand hanging around the house waiting for nothing to happen. There was no point in going to school, and after a while there are few variations of "It'll be all right" before you feel that the script has simply run out.

There was no sound from Mr. Thomas's workshop. But the padlock hung loose from the hasp, so I gave the door a more confident rap than I felt.

There were a couple of seconds' silence and then the door

pushed open and he stood looking down at me, as if annoyed at being interrupted. There was a paintbrush in his right hand, and the smell of varnish hung in the air.

"Ah, Graham, isn't it?" he said. "Well, come in. What can I do for you?"

"That's difficult, Mr. Thomas. It's a complicated story —"

"Well, take a seat — there, grab that stool. Yes that's it. You don't mind if I carry on with this, do you? Don't want to leave a brush mark by stopping and starting."

He went back to painting the body of the horse, stroking the wet varnish into the wood.

"Mr. Thomas," I said, conscious that within minutes he'd be throwing me out of his shed with a curse.

"Mr. Thomas, my father was arrested during the night."

He carried on with his work, dipping the brush into the can and carefully following the grain.

"The police say that he released secret information about the StarRaider project on the Internet and that he's being charged under the Official Secrets Act."

He refreshed his brush, listening. I looked around the workshop, noticing for the first time the several carved heads that hung on the wall at the back, waiting to be attached to bodies.

Silence filled the air like dust.

He said, turning around, "I'm sorry to hear about your dad — uh, Graham — but what has this got to do with me?"

"Mr. Thomas," I started again. "You've visited our house and you know the kind of people we are. Do you think it likely that my dad would have done such a thing?"

He finished the right hind leg, wiped the varnish from the

brush, and then placed it in a jar of water. He took a cloth, poured some turpentine onto it, and rubbed his hands.

"Do you think I had something to do with this, uh, criminal act?"

"I don't know, Mr. Thomas. I — I think you might know more than you're saying to me."

I thought at that moment he was going to lose his temper, that he would start shouting and that I'd have simply wasted my time and caused more trouble. And that the police would be wanting to know why I'd interfered with the investigation.

"Let me see," he said, leaning against the doorjamb. "You'll have noticed, I expect, the special way I have of smiling?" He pointed to the curious, lopsided twist to his face.

"I wasn't born like that, Graham. It wasn't some kind of genetic inheritance from my mam or dad. But I was lucky. I was caught by a high-velocity round from a rifle. The bullet clipped a muscle as it passed by at twenty-two hundred feet a second. My pal, standing next to me, wasn't so fortunate. The metal that caught him took away a vertebra at the base of his spine. Took him to the ground quicker than an axed tree.

"And the pathetic thing was, as he lay in the mud, he tried to get up. The top half of his body straining to make his legs work. But of course they didn't, because communications traffic from base headquarters had been severed.

"He got a good pension and waltzes around in a super-duper wheelchair and everything, but you see, it's not the same. Not with his being a football player and athlete. Kind of spoiled that.

"That was all years ago, in the Falklands — during the war

between Britain and Argentina in the eighties. The crazy thing about it was that my pal was hit with a bullet manufactured in London, and I expect that I was grazed by metal machined in the same place."

"But —" I began.

"I mean, years ago the people who made the swords and the bows and the arrows, they were probably familiar with the effects of their craft. They knew that if you hit someone hard enough with a sword, you'll take an arm clean away, chop a great wedge out of a body, but if you're in front of a monitor all day — well, you might as well be putting together the code for a games machine."

"Mr. Thomas," I said again, "I understand all this. He was working on software for a European defense aircraft. It wasn't designed for export, as far as I know. Simply to protect Britain against invaders."

He looked at me sharply and then pulled a handkerchief from his pocket and blew his nose.

"You don't believe that, do you?"

He spoke softly, and at that moment I felt a great surge of emotion, like a rising tide that had been held back.

"No," I said quietly.

"Things are difficult for all of us, Graham," he said eventually. "But when you see great wrongs being done and stand aside, surely you're as guilty as the person committing that offense?"

He paused and rubbed his eyes, as if trying to get something straight.

"Look, you're a young man, and I know that you're acting

as the local attorney on behalf of your father. I know that he's a clever man and that he was hired by the company to provide the brains for this wonderful airplane.

"But I haven't much to say that will be of comfort to you, Graham. Your dad sold his skills on the market. The technology he was working on will be used to kill people in the Third World — mums and dads, aunties and uncles, babies and children — thousands of miles from comfy New Barton."

And at that moment, as we talked in the cold of his workshop, I got the feeling that Mr. Thomas had been through all these arguments before. The bullet that had caught his face in the Falklands War, the round fired by the Argentine soldier, had been made in Britain and was still hurtling through the air. Last night it had struck Dad.

"Some version of that airplane will be exported to a dictator abroad who will use it to slaughter whoever happens to be the particular enemy at the time. Who can say that it's wrong to try and stop that?"

He picked up the can of varnish and carefully replaced the lid.

"There's nothing I can do for you, Graham," he said.

Twenty-five

Violet Thompson was short and heavily stooped, and she took ages getting to the front door of her house. I could hear the slow shuffle and pause as she came down the corridor.

Her hair was thin and pure white and her eyes blue and direct.

"Yes, what is it?" she asked, looking up at me.

"Miss Thompson, my name's Graham Hayton."

"Ah, the boy who's doing the research? You'd better come in."

I hadn't planned to stay. Everything was turned around at home, and I didn't think afternoon tea was going to be a strong possibility. Yet if she'd been busy making seedcake, then the least I could do was stop by and explain something of the situation.

The house was a small two-bedroom affair. Red brick mixed with flint, as was the local custom.

I followed her instruction and placed my jacket on a hook in the hall and then went into the living room — a tiny area filled with books and framed watercolors. There was a brisk fire burning and just room for a couple of armchairs and a coffee table.

"I'm not expecting you at this time, am I?" she asked anxiously, as if concerned that the cold fingers of dementia had touched her world.

"No, no. I'm due at half past four, Miss Thompson, but there's been a — well — a disaster at home and — well — I have to be on hand to help out should the need arise."

"But you'll take a cup of tea?"

"Yes. Thanks."

On any other day I'd have been less abrupt, less withdrawn. I found the effort of making conversation as hard as running any cross-country race against the clock. All the time I was in that small house — which smelled of old flowers and furniture polish — I was also wondering what was going on at home.

I followed her into the kitchen and for several minutes, as we waited for the kettle to boil, listened to her talk about her house and the village and the research she had once completed. She used to teach in the old school, and the pamphlet on New Barton was the first project of her retirement.

"You see, there weren't any recreation centers or aerobics classes in those days, fortunately, so I was quite happy to check parish records and interview people through newspaper advertisements. I know that it's not very substantial, but it took me the best part of two years to put together.

"I had a couple of hundred copies printed and sold about half that number through the bookshop in Craybourne. If I'd had more money, I'd have included some photographs of the people I met and the buildings I described."

She paused and sipped from her cup.

"And you're living in Sentinel House, you say?"

"Yes. We moved in last October."

"You said there'd been some disaster at home. Not tragic, I hope?"

"No. Not tragic. But, well — it's difficult to explain, Miss Thompson."

"That's all right, dear. It's none of my business. But perhaps I can help you with your interest in Sentinel House," she said, and she reached under the coffee table and pulled out a faded blue folder.

"After I published my pamphlet on the village, several people wrote, saying how much they'd enjoyed the work. Sometimes they corrected mistakes I'd made, and sometimes they provided additional bits of information — just in case I might consider bringing out another edition.

"Well, although I did think about putting together a revised version of the history, I never got around to it. The original impulse seems to have died, and it was never done. But — and more to the point of your visit — about a year after the pamphlet was in circulation, I received a letter from an Elizabeth Holroyd in Beauminster. She'd been sent the pamphlet by her daughter, who lived in our part of the world.

"Elizabeth was well into her eighties at that time, but she had once worked as a serving maid in the kitchen at Sentinel House when it was the Provost Marshal's headquarters, and furthermore, she was courting a sergeant who worked up the hill at the old camp."

At this point she opened the file and turned over several sheets of lined paper until she came to an envelope.

"This is what I think you might find of interest in your research," she said, and she passed the envelope over, commenting, "It was a sad business."

The writer had used a ballpoint pen and had been taught to write in the old-fashioned manner — all loops and curves. But over the years, the style had deteriorated and become ragged, like an old hedge that had been neglected and allowed to develop its own outgrowths and wild shape. Consequently, it was sometimes difficult to get the meaning of a passage, and I found myself reading whole pages over again in order to pick up the narrative.

This extract commences halfway down the third page:

I was appointed kitchen maid in the Provost Marshal's office at Sentinel House in the autumn of 1917.

The soldiers were known as redcaps on account of the distinctive band they wore on their uniform hats. They served as the army's police force.

In the early part of 1918 a soldier was brought into Sentinel House and imprisoned in one of the basement cells. I can remember this quite clearly because he was the subject of a lot of talk by the officers in the place, and we gathered that he'd committed a serious offense and that he was to be put on trial for it — a court-martial, in fact.

He was served meals like everyone else, the food being taken down to him by the duty guard. Then one day, sometime in February, I would have thought, I was asked to make a seed-cake for the prisoner. The cook was ill at the time, and I remember most particular that the cake had to be ready by teatime on a Wednesday.

Well, that wasn't a great hardship, although I thought it odd that a fellow who had been locked away for the past month and given a mighty plain diet might now be indulged with a most particular confection.

To get to the point, the cake was made and he was given a slice on the Wednesday, as per instruction, and then, to my surprise, he vanished from the place.

"What is the prisoner having for lunch?" I asked the next day, and I was told that he'd left.

Well, in time of war, you got used to odd things happening. Your job was to carry out orders and do your duty.

Shortly after this, that Easter, I started courting with a sergeant from the camp, Frank Holroyd. He never liked to talk about his work, but years after, when we'd been married and had two babies with a third on the way, Frank told me about an incident that had taken place during the war.

He felt bad about what had happened, and as he told the story he had difficulty in containing his emotion.

All the soldiers were roused at seven one morning and made to stand around three-quarters of the parade ground. A further platoon of nine stood within the square, with their rifles in the shoulder position.

Soon a truck drove up, and two men jumped down from the back and dragged a third onto the ground. Frank said that they were none too gentle with this creature, but treated him as if he were a particularly troublesome bag of spuds.

This third soldier had his hands tied behind him, and he was led, head down, onto the parade ground, so that all the assembled could see his plight.

Frank said that everyone was filled with foreboding at this, because they recognized that the prisoner was Private Whitaker, who had until recently been one of their number and was friendly with several.

When young Whitaker was situated at the open end of the square, next to a wooden chair placed for the purpose, the Sergeant Major brought the company to attention, and one of the officers addressed the parade.

He told them that it was his duty to communicate the sentence of the recent court-martial held on Private Whitaker and to ensure that it was carried out to the satisfaction of the law and in favor of military discipline.

Well, the upshot was that Whitaker had been sentenced to death by firing squad for betraying his country and that this sentence had been confirmed by various generals and bigwigs in the army. There was no court of appeal or anything like that.

They dragged Whitaker to the chair and quickly bound him hand and foot, dropped a black bag over his head, and pinned a piece of white cloth to his chest.

The nine soldiers who had come equipped with rifles took their aim and at the signal of the officer — he brought down his swagger stick — fired a volley into the heart of the young man.

Frank said that the force of the bullets ripping into his body *knocked him sideways and that he continued to jerk and move for some minutes after the spirit had passed from him.*

And as he lay there, covered in blood, the Colonel told the men that justice had been done and that this was to be seen as a warning to anyone else who had treasonous thoughts in their mind.

By comparing times and dates it was obvious that the young man who had been imprisoned at Sentinel House was the same Paul Whitaker who had been so brutally killed up on the hill.

I believe that his grave can be found in the churchyard at Tydeworth camp.

Frank told me that it was the most disgraceful act he witnessed during his three years in the army and that it made him ashamed to wear the King's uniform.

As I sat there with the letter in my hand before Miss Thompson and that roaring fire, I thought back over the various moments during those few weeks that winter. I thought back over the events that had taken place eighty years before and wondered yet again how far the past had stretched out a hand to touch the present. I thought, too, of those words we'd uncovered in the cellar:

To be aware of the suffering of fellow creatures, to be a help-mate in the cause of death, is an abomination I could endure no longer, and I gave witness to what I knew.

Twenty-six

"Mr. Hayton, I wonder if you might glance over this document. Now, could you explain to the court what we are looking at?"

"It's a copy of the Official Secrets Act."

"Ah. And what is that?"

"It's a law designed to safeguard the security of the country."

" 'To safeguard the security of the country!' Exactly so, Mr. Hayton. The Official Secrets Act is signed by people who work in secret areas. By signing it they promise not to reveal those secrets to anyone else. Isn't that so, Mr. Hayton?"

"Yes."

"And were the severe penalties for breaking the Act explained to you?"

"Yes."

"Yes. So why did you have to sign the document when you took your job at Spere Electronics?"

"Because I was involved in designing computer software that was being developed for use in an advanced fighter aircraft."

"And the British government — and other European governments for that matter — wouldn't want information about this aircraft — technical information about how it flies — to be widely known?"

"No."

"So would you like to tell the court how such technical information was made available on the Internet? How it could be accessed by *anyone* plugging into a Web site called — uh — Lamplight? And how your own e-mail address was given as the contact for further inquiries?"

"I don't know. I never passed on any information over the Internet. Or made copies of classified inform —"

"But you have already pleaded guilty to breaking one section of the Official Secrets Act: you've already told this court that you were in the habit of taking computer disks home."

"Yes, but —"

"And the e-mail address publicized on the Internet is yours?"

"Yes."

"What I wonder, Mr. Hayton, is how you can still maintain your innocence?"

We had to wait five months for the trial at Craybourne Crown Court. Five months before the press recorded the way the prosecution's Roger Carlyle tore gaping wounds in Dad's defense. I was a mere fifty yards from him while all this was going on. It might have been a thousand miles. I sat on a bench outside Court Number 2, watching the black movement of clerks and lawyers.

"It's because you're a defense witness, young man," said Mr. Bellamy, puffing on his cigar. "Got to wait your turn."

The press had arrived immediately after the news broke about Dad's arrest.

I'd just gotten to the bend on Potters Road, before our house, when I saw the parked cars and groups of people in front of the fence. A film crew was unloading from the side of a van, and a blond woman came out of the gate. Even from a distance I could hear their chatter and laughter. Several were drinking from thermoses, and a man in a leather jacket was eating a sandwich as he talked to his friend.

They stopped what they were doing as I pedaled up the road. Then there was the lightning of flash bulbs, and someone pushed a microphone into my face.

"It's Graham, isn't it?" said a man with a short beard and thin face, and someone grabbed my arm, and a third called out, "What do you know about your dad, Graham?" and "Do you think he's a spy?"

And then I broke free and ran the bike down the side of the house, shaking off further shouts like a cloud of summer flies.

"They've been here for the last hour," said Mum. "I've had to turn on the answering machine because of the number of calls we're getting. We've been offered thousands of pounds by the newspapers to tell our story."

Matty was at the kitchen table, listening. She had a book open and was messily coloring a picture of a farmyard.

"Is there any —"

"News?" Mum interrupted, moving to the sink to fill the kettle. "Yes. Plenty. It's the main item on TV and radio. There's even been a statement from the American government saying that they have every confidence that Britain will deal with this serious breach of security."

"Daddy didn't do anything wrong," said Matty, biting her tongue in concentration. "He's a — a good man."

"No, I didn't —"

"I know — forgive me," Mum said, coming across the kitchen and touching my arm. "You wondered if we'd heard from the police, not whether we're on the news."

She leaned against the cabinet by the stove.

"You know, Graham, I haven't had a cigarette in sixteen years, but if one of those goons" — and she gestured toward the front of the house — "came in and offered me one, I think I'd smoke the whole pack."

I let the silence gather, so that all we could hear was the steady scrape of Matty's markers. I never really thought about it then, but on reflection I suppose Matty was comforting herself, working on an activity that would keep demons away.

"We can see Dad at six o'clock this evening. Arthur Bellamy says that he's going to appear before a judge this afternoon and that the police are likely to oppose bail."

"Which means —" I began.

Mum shut me up with a look. Although events were unraveling at frightening speed, she still wanted to protect Matty from the certainty that Dad was going to spend the next few months locked in a cell while awaiting trial.

*   *   *

That lunchtime, we sat and stirred tomato soup around in our bowls. It was as though all our lives had been suspended, like we'd taken a wrong turn somewhere and found ourselves facing a brick wall, unable to get back to the main road.

At one point Mum leapt up from her seat, yanked the back door open, and ran out, shouting to a photographer, "Get out of our garden. If you trespass again I'll call the police."

And all the time, Matty sat quietly, nibbling a piece of bread and sipping her soup. She spoke only once; when Mum came back inside and closed the door, she asked, "Will Daddy be coming home soon?"

We were at the police station in Craybourne a bit before ten of six. While Mum went down a brightly lit corridor with a police officer, Matty and I waited in Interview Room 2. It was very cramped and bare: a small table and three chairs; the walls covered in writing. In some bizarre way it reminded me of the hut in the camp at Wilson's Wood. The place was stamped with unhappiness and desperation, a place where people tried to lie their way back to freedom.

After about half an hour, and after I'd read Matty a couple of picture books, we were led down a corridor and into room 32. Dad rose as we entered and clutched at Matty, who rushed to wrap her arms around him. He looked at me over the top of Matty's head, and I could see that he was trying to control his emotions — you know, the ones that are pressing you to cry, but you realize you mustn't, so that the effort robs you of speech and leaves you with an ache in your throat.

"Daddy's all right," said Mum, standing up from her chair next to the table. "They've been very nice to him, and Mr. Bellamy has arranged for a special lawyer to come down from London so that Daddy can come home as soon as possible."

We didn't stay long, and not a lot was said. Dad worked hard to ask us questions and made jokes about the journalists and photographers, but you could see that he was exhausted after the sleepless night, the hours of questioning, the shock of the arrest. The fact that his tie had been taken away was a reminder that he was no longer able to do as he wished.

And so the months passed.

Bail was opposed. We were all interviewed by the police — including Matty — and as winter thawed into spring and the days lengthened to summer, Dad was kept in a cell at Borough Bridge Prison.

Sometimes Mum went to see him on her own, sometimes all three of us drove the thirty miles across Hampshire. They were long, miserable months. After the first weeks of press interest and an explosion of fascination at school, a kind of dreary routine took over. Lesson followed lesson, and although I would occasionally go and chat with Mr. Pyatt, each day school slid farther down on my list of priorities. I sometimes saw John Franklin, but I had no interest in chewing the fat at break, even less in going over on weekends.

Each Tuesday and Saturday we could see Dad. Thursday night we all went to the supermarket, and on Sundays we helped clean the house.

Because Dad's salary had been frozen by Spere (until the

result of the trial was known), Mum put her name on the county list of substitute teachers. Several days a week she dropped Matty off at a baby-sitter's in the village and then hurtled down the highway to whichever high school had hired her services.

Of all of us, I think Matty took the sudden disappearance of Dad the hardest. She would call out in the night complaining of a stomachache or would wake up screaming from a nightmare. Often she would go into Mum's room before six, crying that she didn't like Mrs. Hilliard, the baby-sitter, and that the other kids were nasty to her at school.

I suppose with everything else going on, it was natural that Mum should seek help from our family physician, who referred us to Dr. Davies at the family guidance clinic.

That side of it — talking to the psychologist — didn't really bother me at the time. I think Mum and I were too tuned in to the possibility that not only had Dad been suspended by Spere but that he was facing years in prison.

Twenty-seven

"I am innocent because I *never* transmitted the source codes or anything else relating to the StarRaider on the Internet."

"And yet, according to the witness statement obtained from your managing director, Mr. Fletcher, there are aspects of the code that only *you* were working on. Isn't that so?"

"Yes."

"So, Your Honor, ladies and gentlemen of the jury, the information that found its way onto the Internet could only have been produced by Mr. Hayton. No one else had access to the work. And no one else had the same e-mail address.

"No further questions, Your Honor."

The trial had started at ten that morning in May. We'd left home early because of road construction just before the Shaftesbury junction and arrived with forty minutes to spare.

Mum and I had few words to say as we followed the stop-and-go taillights into Craybourne. There had been a mention of the trial on the nine o'clock news, and I suspect an outline of the case appeared in most of the newspapers, but none of us were interested in what the press had to say. A resentful Matty, clutching her pink rabbit, was dropped off at Mrs. Hilliard's.

Mr. Bellamy had hired a Christopher Dyer from London to act as our defense attorney.

"He'll do a thorough job, Mrs. Hayton," Mr. Bellamy said the week before the trial. "It's not as bad as you might think." And he patted Mum's arm as he showed us to the door.

He'd spent the session explaining the rules that would operate throughout the trial so that we could understand what was going on during the various stages. It was very much like a play, with everyone cast in different roles taking turns to perform in character.

The serious questioning of Dad by the prosecution occurred on the afternoon of the first day. It had followed statements by Dad's boss, Mr. Fletcher, and by a Mr. Simon Glover, who had been introduced to the court as an expert witness for the prosecution. His job was to show the jury how the magic of the Internet worked — how you got the genie out of the bottle, so to speak.

I suppose for the audience in that legal theater it would have been great entertainment — after the prosecution buildup — to actually *see* what the crime looked like on a Web site halfway around the world, but for me it wasn't great TV, since I knew that Exhibit A had the power to destroy my life.

According to Mum, speaking to me over a dinner that neither of us ate, Glover was a young man in his twenties who wore his hair in a ponytail.

"It sat on his shoulders," she said, "like a dead rat." He had a thin voice and a cough that broke up his speech.

"He wasn't called right away," she said. "The prosecution wanted a short adjournment. A couple of men came in and put up a screen and pushed in the electronic boxes — you know, the PC and projector and so forth." She looked away, staring out through the kitchen window to the garden wall and the ivy glistening in the pale light.

"The prosecution's attorney Mr. Carlyle said that he wanted the jury to see for themselves how the Internet worked. How easy it was to send messages to the States.

"Then of course they brought in the weedy Simon Glover, who had to be reminded on two occasions to speak up because the court microphone wasn't recording what he was saying."

Again she stopped, and I was conscious of how worn — how frayed — she looked. The fading light didn't help, but her gray eyes shone like broken glass and her lipstick had leached into her skin.

I guess the jury must have been really wired by the time Mr. Carlyle put Glover through his paces. They'd pulled up a search engine as a start, and then, before going any further, Carlyle turned to the jury and said, "So let us see, ladies and gentlemen of the jury, what the work of a traitor looks like. Indeed, let us see where the top-secret information entrusted to the care of Brian Hayton ended up. Could you please type in *StarRaider?*"

I could only imagine the dry-mouthed anticipation that would have met that request, people straining in their seats to get a better look at the screen.

And then, of course, three or four seconds later, the handful of options appeared, including:

Development

Government policy

History

and

Operating codes

And then, after allowing the tension to stretch a little, Carlyle said, "Operating codes."

There was complete silence in court during this sequence of events, and nobody spoke when the following text, blue on white, flashed across four thousand miles and hung a guilty sign on the screen in Court Number 2. For the secret that Lamplight gave to the world went like this: "The following lines contain source code for the StarRaider avionics system. This information has been made available to the public in the interest of world peace. For an update contact: hayton@sentinel. boulder.co.uk."

There then appeared lines and lines and lines of what might have been hieroglyphics.

The binary black magic.

Twenty-eight

We had to wait until the third day for our interrogation.

It was one of those typically English spring mornings — not clear blue skies, swallows, and cowslips, but think wads of cloud, steady rain, and traffic stalled on the highway. I sat in the back of the car next to Matty, rereading Dad's letter. It had been written on Monday night, and when I look at it now, I can feel once again the sense of foreboding — that the earnest hope expressed would not be fulfilled. It wasn't a comfort as we crawled into Craybourne. It added to the misery, because I guess it emphasized everything that might be thrown away.

Dear Graham,

I'm not in a position to talk to you as I would have liked, but I want to apologize for getting you involved in this drama. I'm quite sure that you'll just be asked to talk about the time you and Matty were locked in the cellar — and of course the prosecution will want you to say that I brought the wretched computer disks home on a regular basis. Just tell the truth in your own way, and I know the jury will believe in what they hear.

This has been a terrible — frightening — experience for us all, although I'm quite sure that at some stage we'll be able to look back and find some value in it.

During these past few months I've had plenty of time to think about our lives — the good and the not so wonderful. And I suppose that now mine has been put on hold, I can regret lost opportunities.

When I was a child I went with a friend to a nearby railroad crossing, and for whole days during one summer we spent our time collecting the numbers of passing trains. Somewhere in the attic you'll find those notebooks.

I confess that I can still remember the sense of excitement I felt when we heard the whine of the rails before the gate swung across the road. And then the rush of the passing train. At the end of the day, there were all those pages filled with neat columns of numbers and a sense of a job well done.

It was like ordering the world into a comfortable, controllable shape.

I've never thought back to that time until today, when Mr. Glover called up the Web site and we could see the lines of computer code that had come from my disks. As I looked at the screen, I couldn't help wondering whether I hadn't spent my life waiting for passing trains.

This is a bit deep, but perhaps if I'm given a second chance

*we might go to Stamford Bridge together and see the greatest
team in the world do their stuff.*

With love,
Your Dad

As everyone now knows, Matty was interviewed after lunch on
Wednesday afternoon. Mr. Bellamy and Mr. Dyer felt that her
testimony about what had happened during our afternoon in
the cellar would appeal to the jury. There had never been a dis-
pute about the incident, but Matty's innocence would add
credibility to the case: she would speak the truth.

Because of her age it was arranged for her to sit with Mum
in a counseling room and be videotaped with a colleague of
Mr. Dyer's. The interview was to be transmitted live into the
court.

But this was later after my own ordeal under cross-examination.

Although Mr. Bellamy had explained how everything worked
in the court days before the trial opened, having to sit in the
long corridor that Wednesday morning, watching and not seeing the cars filtering through onto the Shaftesbury road, I
think I would have changed places with the greasy youth beg-
ging for coins in the underpass.

For forty minutes I had to wait, without knowing when the
pale door into the large room would swing back and the sum-
mons to take the stand would be made. Having to tell my story
according to the ritual of question and answer; aware of Mum
in the visitors' area; the cluster of lawyers and clerks; the curi-

ous jury opposite; the press behind; the judge, Mr. Wingate, to my left. And to my right, his face stretched and gray, my father.

But then suddenly it was "Mr. Hayton?," and I was in the witness box, and repeating after the clerk the words: "I swear by almighty God that the evidence I shall give be the truth, the whole truth, and nothing but the truth."

And later still, once I had explained to Mr. Dyer what had taken place in the cellar, I stood looking at the face of the prosecuting counsel, Mr. Roger Carlyle, who rose thoughtfully from his chair and approached with a frown creasing his forehead.

"Mr. Hayton," he began. "You have told the jury that on the afternoon of the sixth of December last year you went down into the cellar of your house. Is that correct?"

"Yes."

"How long were you in the cellar, with your sister, Mathilda, before you heard the sound of someone walking through your house. Approximately, of course."

A flicker of a smile crossed his face. I thought back to that time and thought of this: Where was the snag in the question? What could I say that would lead to danger?

I gave up. "Five minutes or so, I would think." And then: "It wasn't very long because I hadn't found the light switch, which is attached to one of the beams. In the roof of the cellar."

"Fine. Five minutes. And then what happened?"

"Well, I think it was Matty — Mathilda — my sister — she heard the sound of footsteps."

"And where were they coming from — when you first heard them?"

I was standing on the brick floor of the cellar, smelling the damp and feeling the cold touch of fear as those feet came across the tiles from the back of the house to where we were standing. Both of us looking up. At some point Matty's hand crept into mine.

"From the kitchen. That is, from the back of the house. They came toward us."

"And —?"

"And then stopped by the door of the cellar. We'd left it open."

"You said in your statement to the police that the person then closed the door and locked you both in — and in fact it wasn't until your parents returned home three hours later that you were released?"

"Yes."

"Mr. Hayton" — and at this point Carlyle looked down at the sheaf of papers he was carrying — "do you recall what the weather was like that weekend — the weekend of the fifth and sixth of December?"

"Yes. It had snowed on the Saturday. Well, on the Friday night. I can remember because we'd gone into Craybourne shopping on the Saturday."

"And on the Sunday, what was the ground like? Can you remember?"

That morning I'd gone out with John Franklin bike-riding along the path on the hill above the farm. I could remember the mud and puddles and slush.

"It was wet. There had been a bit of a thaw, so there was slush around. The ground was pretty muddy."

"'The ground was pretty muddy,'" Carlyle repeated, pausing as if I'd said something of significance. And he turned to the jury. "It's worth noting, ladies and gentlemen of the jury, that no trace of water or mud was found in the Haytons' house when the police arrived. And furthermore, there was no evidence of forced entry into the building. The burglary becomes more and more mysterious. But that's not all, of course.

"Mr. Hayton. Your father brought his work home with him?"

"Yes. He was dedicated to the — the — StarRaider project."

"And on at least one occasion he showed you computer disks that were to be used in the aircraft?"

"Yes. Yes, he did."

"Were those disks distinctive in any way?"

Silence.

In court, in the air-conditioned cool, you couldn't even hear the sound of people in the corridor outside. Just rows of faces. Pale wood. Recessed lights.

"The disks I saw, once, they had a red strip along the bottom."

"'A red strip along the bottom.'" Again that ironic repetition of what I'd said. "Like this, for instance?" And he went over to his table, opened a document file, and pulled out a black disk with the colored marking.

"Yes."

"And did your father leave disks like this in his study?"

"No." I felt more confident now. Felt like I was on sure ground. "No. The only time he ever showed us the StarRaider disks, he replaced them in a special case. They were locked with some kind of security device."

"And you never saw disks like these in his study?"

"No."

"And when the police arrived that evening, did your father say to them that there had been a security problem? That he had left material around that was valuable or sensitive in some way?"

"No."

"So it's unlikely that information on the StarRaider disks — computer code and so on — could have been sent on the Internet that afternoon?"

I could see where he was coming from now. If the intruder hadn't sent the information, then Dad must have done it. I was helping Mr. Carlyle chisel out a verdict of guilty. Because if the intruder hadn't e-mailed Lamplight, who had?

"Mr. Hayton?"

The judge, Mr. Wingate, stopped writing and looked over his desk.

"I'm sorry?"

"Without the StarRaider disks, Mr. Hayton, could the information have been sent by the burglar?"

"No," I wiped sweat from my forehead. "No. It couldn't."

"Thank you. No further questions."

Twenty-nine

"What do you think, Mr. Bellamy?"

We were in a plain room on the first floor of the court. A single barred window looked out onto an inner enclosure, and Dad sat behind a table looking at the rotund solicitor pulling off the plastic from a package of cheap cigars. His open brief-case and three colored folders were piled on the table.

"Not a disaster, Brian, by any means. I've just —"

"Mr. Bellamy, I'm not an idiot."

In the white light Dad's face was pale and gaunt. There was a tension about him that spread out from the screwed-up intensity of his eyes and the tightness of his mouth.

"I know it's your job to keep my spirits up —"

The solicitor raised his hand.

"Right. Listen. You haven't been found guilty of the main charge. The prosecution has presented the court with a series of facts, but these are all circumstantial. You have acknowledged that you took the disks home. It's not in doubt that the information got on the Internet — but there's nothing to prove 'beyond a reasonable doubt' that *you* were responsible for e-mailing Lamplight."

There was comfort in Mr. Bellamy's assurance with his friendliness and confidence. After all, I can remember thinking, he must know what he's doing.

Toward the end of the meeting, Mr. Dyer, our lawyer, came in. He looked different out of his wig, more like a normal person, I suppose, than someone who had just flown in from the eighteenth century.

He was a tall man with receding dark hair and a prominent Adam's apple. He spoke with the voice, the accent, of someone who had grown up learning Latin and Greek at some top private school.

After he had shaken hands and said hello, he surprised us all by adding to Mr. Bellamy's aura of confidence.

"Not a bad morning," he said, smiling. "The prosecution has a problem: it hasn't got a plausible theory as to why you, Brian, should have suddenly taken it into your head to give away state secrets.

"Gone bonkers? No evidence. Given large dollops of money by an enemy power? No evidence. Got a sudden conscience about working for the arms industry? The cupboard is bare.

"All they can say is that a crime has been committed, but they can do no more than suggest that you are *one* of the suspects. The cross-examination of Graham was pretty desperate stuff," he added, and he squeezed my arm reassuringly.

When we returned to court that afternoon, officials were busy putting up a screen and sorting out television cables. The lawyers clustered in groups discussing — for all I know — their plans for the next weekend, while the reporters chatted and laughed and my immediate neighbors talked about sicknesses and vacations.

Dad presumably reflected on his life.

And then the clerk of the court brought an abrupt silence with "The court will come to order," and Mr. Dyer was on his feet.

"I am grateful for the court's indulgence while we got the technical arrangements in place. You have heard, ladies and gentlemen of the jury, that the prosecution has maintained throughout that the defendant, Mr. Hayton, was responsible for sending technical information about the new aircraft to a Web site in the United States." He paused and looked down, as if to give the jury time to get up to speed.

"We listened this morning to the evidence of Matty's brother about what took place on the afternoon of the sixth of December, when the children were locked in the cellar of their house. But what of Matty herself? What was her experience on that crucial afternoon? And, more important, what did she notice?

"My learned friend, Mrs. Sturridge, will pick up the story with Matty."

At that point Matty's face suddenly ballooned into the courtroom. Light flooded away behind her, and, probably from some signal, she looked up from the drawing she was plainly doing and stared into the camera.

It was at this moment that I could see the point of using her as a defense witness. How could someone so young and so innocent tell anything but the truth?

"Matty?" said a voice, presumably that of Mrs. Sturridge, "I'd like to talk to you about your house."

Matty's head was bent, her right hand scrubbing away at some paper.

"Do you remember that time when you and Graham went into the cellar?"

"When we — when the door was — ?" She looked to her right. "When we was — shut in?"

"When you were shut in."

"It was cold. Do you wear a funny hat — like the other people?"

"Sometimes, Matty. But not now."

"When we were in the cellar we heard the steps. They went into Daddy's room."

She bent and scribbled away busily for a second. "They were using Daddy's computer."

Silence.

"How do you know that, Matty?"

"Because" — and she looked up into the camera, her eyebrows drawn in concentration — "because I heard that funny sound the computer makes when Daddy looks up Chelsea."

"What do you mean 'that funny sound'?"

"You know — like a telephone noise." And she giggled, and then said, "It goes — kind of — beep — bip — beep — beep — beep."

Again I was back in the cold light of last winter, listening to the silence overhead and then crossing the cellar to mount the stairs and check the door. And while I was gone, in those thirty seconds, Matty heard that strange slurry of high-frequency sound coming from the computer. And she knew what it meant.

"Was the person using the Internet, Matty?"

She didn't say anything for ten seconds, and I think everyone must have thought that she hadn't heard or didn't understand the question. But then, looking very serious, she replied, "I think so. I thought that it was Paul — Paul Whitaker again. But I knew that Paul wouldn't — wouldn't hurt us. You know?"

There was silence.

"The person that came into the house locked the door. That person wasn't Paul." Pause. "Do you like my picture?"

"Matty," said Mrs. Sturridge quietly. "Who is Paul?"

There was a long, long silence. Everyone in the court looked at the screen as though it was the last thirty seconds of a Hollywood movie.

"Paul lived in the house — years and years and years ago." She stopped and thought for a moment. "He was *Private* Paul Whitaker. He isn't alive anymore. He tried to stop people — he tried to stop bad men making — poisonous gas."

"So —"

"They took him away — up the hill and tied him to a chair. They said bad things about him and — covered his face. And then other men pointed their guns. And they shot him — as he sat there. That morning."

"He's" — Matty looked into the camera again — "he's a ghost."

Thirty

On my desk there's an old book, a pocket watch that's stopped at eleven minutes past five, and three old coins.

I can hear Matty in the garden playing with her friend Susan. They've spread a crib blanket on the grass. Their dolls are having a picnic.

Mum has gone over to visit Violet Thompson in the village, and she's left the radio on in the kitchen. The to and fro of voices tells me some polite talk program is being broadcast.

When Matty's face had been turned off, silence was switched on in the court. The judge — Mr. Wingate — defense attorney, assembled lawyers and court officials, reporters and jury, and the three rows of people in the visitor's gallery were motionless — unmoving and unspeaking. Dad sat with his head in his hands.

Amid the clutter on my desk there's a torn newspaper clipping from the *Express,* the day after Matty's evidence: *Ghost Haunts Trial* says the headline, and below there's a photograph of our house, taken in December. The curtains have been closed, and there are tire tracks in the yard. It looks deserted — and secretive.

Over everything hung the presence of Paul Whitaker. During that week, all the newspapers ran features on the plight of conscientious objectors in the First World War. The Ministry of Defense confirmed the existence of Private Whitaker, late of the Wiltshire regiment, and acknowledged that he had received a death sentence at a court-martial in 1918 as a result of a serious breach of security concerning poison gas research.

The Times said they had no record of any correspondence from any Private Whitaker.

And yet while it became a topic for discussion in schools and offices, on radio and TV, we had to live with the continuing drama in Court Number 2 at Craybourne. When we got home that night, we sat at the kitchen table drinking tea. I don't suppose any of us knew where to start, and even Matty was quiet. Mum flipped through the day's paper; Matty nibbled on a cookie; I watched a spider darning its web. You could hear the bad-tempered bickering of magpies outside.

Then Mum closed the paper and spoke to us both.

"This has been a terrible, terrible ordeal. For your father, locked up and shamed; for us, trying to carry on our lives as though nothing has happened." She paused and pinched the bridge of her nose, eyes closed.

"Dad and I were proud of you both. We brought you up to tell the truth, and you did just that.

"I can't pretend to know anything about ghosts or the supernatural, but despite the slippery tongue of the prosecution, we weren't shamed. However awkward the evidence, you didn't let us down."

She stopped talking, bent her head, and cried.

Thirty-one

Craybourne Crown Court is in the center of town, across from the swimming pool and separated from the old woolen mill by a highway.

The court building is no more than ten years old, I guess, constructed from cream-colored stone and with a roof that splits neatly down the ridge to allow light to fall through copious sheets of glass.

I suppose when it was designed, the idea was to demonstrate to the world a sense of balance and fairness about the justice system: the exact divide of the sloping roof suggesting evenhandedness; the light pouring in through the windows bringing to mind honesty and truth.

You can reach the court by the underpass from the swimming-pool parking lot, and it's the place where many people attending a trial choose to leave their cars.

That Friday morning, after we'd bought a ticket for space number 163, we joined the thin foot traffic of swimmers, shoppers, and workers heading away from town in the direction of the seat of justice.

The strange soldier in the mist and the fierce dog that leapt out at us that first night seemed galaxies away as we sat in the gradually filling court and waited for someone to press the FORWARD button.

Mr. Bellamy came over once he'd spotted us and ran through the sequence of events due to unwind during the day. Dad looked up once before the judge appeared and produced a faded smile.

In his summing up for the jury, our lawyer Mr. Dyer was sharp and to the point about the absence of incriminating evidence that might link Dad to the transmission of an e-mail across the Atlantic.

Furthermore, although it was accepted that December 6 was the critical day, Mr. Dyer quietly pointed to the eloquent testimony of Matty — "a small girl with sharp ears who heard the computer dialing signal that meant an e-mail was being sent on a wintery afternoon when her father was far from home."

And as for bringing classified computer disks home, Mr. Hayton had *offered* this fact to the police, and what could be construed from this other than the behavior of a man dedicated to his work and proud of his role in the development of the technology?

Yet, unseen and unsaid, it was the ghost of Paul Whitaker that brooded over the speech. It felt like everyone was waiting for some mention, some reference to the hand of the dead man. That other defendant in that other trial.

It was to be the prosecution who seized this weapon and turned it against us.

Standing tall in his black gown and gray wig, Mr. Roger Carlyle rubbed the side of his expensive red nose and spoke to the jury, touching on the main points of the case, the statements made by the various witnesses, and the claims put forward by the defense, and then said, "This is a perplexing case in many ways. The defense has made great play of the fact that there doesn't appear to be a motive for Brian Hayton's behavior.

"And yet the facts *are* clear. The defendant was working on a top-secret project that involved state-of-the-art computer programming. Strictly against the policy of the company and also against the law of the land . . . he took the programming disks home on numerous occasions and even *boasted* about the project and his role in it to his family.

"This information, to which only he had access, was published on a Web site and the defendant's address included as a point of contact.

"We don't know what motivated Brian Hayton. We don't believe in transients breaking into the house, neighbors with a grudge — or, most improbably, Matty's ghost. That an unfortunate soldier did exist and was imprisoned in Sentinel House many years ago is an interesting fact of history. It is also an interesting fact of law that both Paul Whitaker and Brian Hayton were charged with substantially the same crime.

"Then, as now, betraying the interests of this country was regarded as a highly serious offense. We no longer execute those found guilty of treason, but we do expect them to pay a heavy price for their shameful activities.

"The facts *are* clear, and I would argue, members of the jury, that you have no alternative but to find the defendant guilty as charged."

When the jury was sent out to consider its verdict, we were free to have lunch, wander the corridors of the court, and seek silent comfort from each other. It was as though Dad had died and we were left with memories of the man who had once walked through our lives. The dad who told stories of Brunel, who was hooked on technology, who was consumed by the company who employed him.

And all the time, I felt sick knowing that I might have helped slam the cell door.

That day, as we gathered in the open area on the second floor, the smell of cigar smoke enveloping us, Mr. Bellamy just patted my arm. "Never second-guess a jury, son," he said.

And it was at this time, as we sat miserably on a bench watching the eddies of lawyers and secretaries and journalists, that Matty touched my forearm with her hand, and briefly turned off the ache and the anguish as we waited for the verdict.

At that moment, the normal chatter of words going through my head, the verbal traffic that passes for thought, was filled with a different voice that was not my own.

It was quiet and at first seemed to be coming from a distance — like from the end of a long corridor — but when I concentrated, when I really tuned in, I could hear a young man speaking with a quite clear Wilshire accent. The voice said:

"Come ye blessed of my Father, inherit the kingdom prepared for you from the foundation of the world;

For I was an hungred, and ye gave me meat; I was thirsty and ye gave me drink: I was a stranger, and ye took me in;

Naked, and ye clothed me: I was sick, and ye visited me: I was in prison and ye came unto me."

The jury reentered the court at 2:40 that afternoon.

We sat in the first row in the visitors' area, directly opposite the packed seats of the press gallery. To our right, Dad behind glass; before him, rows of black gowns and wigs; and then, diagonally opposite, the jury filing awkwardly into court. The eighteen-year-old man; the gray-haired woman, the sharply dressed car salesman — and those others who had weighed the evidence for three hours.

"Have you reached a verdict upon which you are all agreed?" asked the clerk, a woman with long hair tied back in a ponytail.

"Yes," said the foreman of the jury, pushing up the bridge of his glasses.

"On the first count, that without lawful authority the defendant disclosed information that had been in his possession, contrary to Section 2 of the 1989 Official Secrets Act, how do you find the defendant?"

The foreman coughed into his hand.

"Not guilty," he said.

Thirty-two

The side door slams below, and the criss-cross chat on the radio ceases: Mum has returned from the village.

"I'm back, Graham. Has everything been all right with Matty and Susan?"

"Fine," I call. "And no phone calls, either."

I can hear the two children below filling up the wading pool in order to bathe their dolls. It's early June, and for two days temperatures have been in the lower seventies. Yesterday the field beyond the wall was filled with the noise of cows as our local farmer pushed them into new pasture. Today it threatens rain — great clods of cumulus clouds have begun to form over Wilson's Wood.

And yet the house is calm. Maybe because night doesn't press against the windows and the events of last winter are finally over; maybe because somewhere a young man who, deprived of his own life, saw the demons driven away in ours and no longer walks the dark.

Despite that, I know this is the hard part, the end of the

story that didn't turn out all right. Not for everybody, because after the excitement of the not-guilty verdict, and the sudden babble of whispered conversation, with reporters quietly leaving the court to phone their news rooms, the judge discharged the jury and then listened as our lawyer Mr. Dyer explained to His Honor why he should look leniently on the defendant when considering a sentence for the lesser charge of taking the computer disks home.

And at length, as the court again drew in its breath, and as Dad stood looking at His Honor across the heads of the attorneys, the judge, Mr. Wingate, said, "Brian Hayton, you have pleaded guilty to failing to take proper care of highly classified information, the result of which is the release to the world of computer codes that lie at the heart of a revolutionary new fighter plane.

"I have listened to testimonials from a variety of people working in the industry who make it clear that you are a clever man who has made a major contribution to British technological development. You are undoubtedly gifted and hardworking and possess the kind of skills that this country clearly has great need to cultivate.

"However, you have also displayed crass stupidity in failing to safeguard the material upon which you had been working and with which you had been entrusted. Years of work and the toil of many others has been wasted because you did not ensure the security of the data in your care. Your enthusiasm for the work and your dedication to the project are not in question, and nor is your loyalty to Britain. However, you knowingly broke Section 8 of the 1989 Official Secrets Act, and you are hereby sentenced to nine months' imprisonment."

This year a pair of swallows has built a nest just above where I sit. They feed their young in rotation, winging backward and forward as the sky changes color and shadows fall across the garden. Mum has planted some herbs underneath the kitchen window, and we have seen hedgehogs most evenings. Over by the wall, where Matty found the badge, there's a clump of stinging nettles and some poppies.

Tomorrow is Tuesday, and we're going to have breakfast early and get into the car and drive to Borough Bridge. And at eleven o'clock the small door of the prison will open, a middle-aged man with wavy hair will emerge — and we'll be together again.

Postscript

The reader has now in his or her possession a more complete version of the facts surrounding the trial of Brian Hayton than might have been found from newspaper reports alone.

The family has since recovered from its ordeal and was anxious to cooperate in the writing of this account. Although Mr. Hayton obviously didn't return to his post at Spere Electronics, he obtained work as a freelance designer of business software.

Matty's distress during the trial of her father gradually eased with his return to the family home and with her acceptance that he wouldn't suddenly be whisked away again.

No one has subsequently been charged with the crime, although the police have kept the file open in the hope of securing a future conviction. It would certainly be libelous to indicate, as a result of my own researches, where I feel the burden of guilt might lie — but the reader is now holding the evidence and is free to speculate.

No one has ever been able to explain satisfactorily Matty's

knowledge of Paul Whitaker, and although skeptics have suggested that she got wind of her brother's research into the circumstances surrounding Whitaker's life and death — and that is what came out during the trial — that doesn't explain the other episodes Graham's story highlights. Nor does it explain the damage to the Hayton home that occurred during the night of December 10 — the very evening when American defense consultants visited Sentinel House.

Could it have been the work of passing vandals who simply decided to give vent to violent feelings on a convenient house? Or, more spectacularly, was this the work of other forces from another time — perhaps that silent army of men shot at dawn throughout the First World War, whose absent names haunt war memorials across Britain?

About the Author

While I was growing up, my father was in the Royal Air Force. This meant that every two years our family would pack up and move to another RAF base. As you can imagine, I had plenty of schools and dozens of friends — most of whom I got to know only briefly.

One of the things that remained constant during my childhood was my regular use of the local library. Even if we ended up in some remote desert air-force station, I always knew that a book could take me into a world filled with people trying to sort out problems often ten times more interesting than my own.

I've written stories and poems since then, some based on things that have happened to me, some on topics that I'm just interested in. The ideas grow from small incidents — people moving to a new house or starting a new school — that can be transformed into something exciting simply by applying the magic question:

"What if — ?"

Nick Manns